SMOKEY
HOLLOW

'Smokey Hollow is fond, funny, indignant and
blessedly unsentimental'

DONAL McCANN

'Hilarious, delightfully irreverent,
I couldn't put it down'

LELIA DOOLAN

'Gleefully irreverent, nostalgic but unsentimental
recall of a time fading'

CYRIL CUSACK

SMOKEY
HOLLOW

A Fictional Memoir

BOB QUINN

THE O'BRIEN PRESS
DUBLIN

First published 1991 by The O'Brien Press Ltd.,
20 Victoria Road, Dublin 6, Ireland.
Copyright text © Bob Quinn
Copyright illustrations, design & typesetting ©
The O'Brien Press Ltd.

10 9 8 7 6 5 4 3 2 1
British Library Cataloguing in Publication Data
Quinn Bob, 1935 - Smokey Hollow
I. Title
823.914 [F]
ISBN 0-86278-269-4

Typeset at The O'Brien Press
Book design: Michael O'Brien
Illustrations (cover & text): Donald Teskey
Separations: The City Office, Dublin
Printing: Billings, Worcester

The O'Brien Press receives assistance from
The Arts Council/An Chomhairle Ealaíon.

It will be worth it, if in the end I manage
To blank out whatever it is that is doing the damage.

THE WINTER PALACE
Philip Larkin

This book is for my children,

including Marcus who missed the last one …

Buíochas do Phádraig

·FOREWORD·

ON CHRISTMAS NIGHT A FEW YEARS AGO I retreated from a noisy television room where James Bond was entertaining my children. I wondered if it might ever be possible to convey to them the world of difference between their childhood and mine. I began to make notes with which to regale them later. Gradually the notes turned into an accumulation of pages, then chapters, until five years later I had a sizable manuscript.

In the process I realised I was playing an irreverent game we had as children which consisted of retouching newspaper photographs – distributing gapped teeth, moustaches, spectacles, crossed eyes and beards indiscriminately on solemn faces.

In this case I was also embellishing and altering: attributing expressions to people whom I had hardly known, describing people I had half-forgotten, inventing characters that never existed. Try as I might I could not narrate remembered incidents and situations in an unvarnished fashion. To apply imagination to the past was infinitely more attractive.

In the end I realised it was impossible, at least for me, to record the literal truth. So much so that when a sibling read the following pages he said we must have grown up in different families. I responded weakly by referring to the play, *Rashomon*, where five different eyewitnesses give utterly contradictory versions of an incident.

This phenomenon is well put in the everyday Gaelic expression, '*Is fíor dhuit*', which, though it sounds like agreement, is in fact a diplomatic reminder that what is true for the goose is not necessarily true for the gander ...

What follows constitutes a memoir which has become the truth for me. Alas, this memoir must also be approached as fiction, a literary form that is a kind of a lie. The best I can hope for is that it is one of those lies that illustrate the truth.

· ONE ·

THE ONLY THING YOU CAN DO WITH BOGEYMEN is pull the covers over your head and wish the night will hurry up so that the daylight can banish them.

You know their shadows are still up there on the ceiling and on the wall. They're peering down, but maybe they won't come near if you hold your breath and don't move, pretend you're already dead, fill your head with things like: Janey Mack me shirt is black, what'll I do for Sunday, go to bed and cover me head, and not get up till Monday. Listen. Not a move. Now I lay me down to sleep I pray the Lord my soul to keep and if I die before I wake I pray the Lord my soul to take. Anything to stop thinking of them. But it's no use; when you've used up all your poems and prayers they're still up there and you're clutching the covers waiting for them to pounce.

Even with his eyes squeezed shut Dominic could always see them plainly. Now one of the shadows was big and black like the huntsman with the hatchet that creeps up on Snow White in the forest because the ugly oul' bitch of a queen has ordered him to kill the girl so that liar of a mirror will be fooled and tell her she's still the fairest of them all. The big dark shadow looms over Snow White and she cringes back. Oh feck, he should have closed his eyes for that bit. He knew it would give him nightmares but he couldn't take his eyes off the screen.

In this nightmare the victim was Bern, his big brother, and the huntsman shadow was his father. Snow White was tied to one of the brass knobs of the bedstead, wriggling like a fish while the huntsman unbuckled his belt. It didn't matter that in the pictures the huntsman was really soft-hearted and let Snow White off with a warning. He got into terrible trouble with the queen that time. He wasn't going to let the next kid off so easy. Dominic huddled deeper into the blankets, examining his conscience, desperately identifying his own sins, wondering which of them would justify him being the next for the hatchet. He heard their mother coming up the stairs at a run. Relief. She'd chase the bogeymen away.

– James, don't. He's learned his lesson.

– I'll learn him more.

The belt thwacked sickeningly against the door jamb as the huntsman practised his swing.

She would be standing at the narrow turn of the stairs, looking through the bannisters. Her eyes would be tired, her face slightly drawn. In her wedding photo in the glass case in the sittingroom she was darkhaired and pretty, but bearing and rearing five children, sewing all their clothes, darning all their socks, keeping the house clean to the exacting standards of her tradition had taken their toll. Dominic would not in the future ever be able to conjure up the sound of her famous silvery laugh because he heard it so rarely. He was more accustomed to sighs or doleful tones as she led the family rosary, the only supplicant to kneel upright.

– He won't do it again, sure you won't, son?

– I'll make damn sure he doesn't.

The belt slapped against the door again. The victim wriggled furiously.

– All I ask is a bit of peace when I get home. All I get is squabbling kids. I'll put an end to it once and for all.

– He's sorry, aren't you, son?

– Yes I am, I am.

He still had not been hit. Abject grovelling was the key to salvation. The anger went from the huntsman shape. The victim went limp.

– I'm warning you, me bucko. Next time you won't have your mother to save you. I'll take your solemn life, I swear.

Bern escaped into bed. Snow White was saved. The huntsman was only pretending, had a heart after all. Dominic raised his head from the covers and peered around the room. The shadows were gone. He heard the parents going downstairs, the third step from the end squeaking as usual, blunting the seriousness of the procession. Before the sittingroom door slammed, Mr Toner called out a final warning.

– Not another sound from any of you.

They waited ten seconds of murmuring from the room below to make sure he wasn't listening at the foot of the stairs to catch them out. Then they relaxed. The reprieved criminal, Bern, made a deprecating sound. His bedmate, Joe, began the whispered interrogation while the youngest listened.

– Did he get you?

– Not at all.

– Go on. He nearly killed you.

– Missed me every time. Couldn't get a decent swipe. He only hit the door. He always does that. He's an oul' softy.

– Didn't sound like it.

– Sure he's only trying to frighten us. Anyway, how would you know? It was me he was aiming at.

One of the girls came on tiptoe from the boxroom.

– Are you all right?

– No thanks to you.

– I only asked, snotty.

– None of your business, anyway. You told him I peed on the cabbages.

– I did not. Mammy saw you herself.

– Only after you told her, you little bitch.

– I'm telling what you called me, you brat.

– Go away, wet your knickers.

– I'm telling on you.

They froze as a door opened and the voice bellowed.

– Go asleep this minute or I'll come up those stairs three at a time. I'll mark you all and that's your last warning.

The sister fled back to her room. There was silence. Since Mr Toner had bored a hole in the ceiling of the room below – to let some of the warm air penetrate upstairs – they had no privacy. It was a well-meant attempt at primitive central heating but it made no difference to the temperature.

Normally he would come up to tuck them in and make the

11

sign of the cross on their foreheads. He would straighten their knees, tell them to sleep on their sides, their arms pillowing their heads in a salute. That's the way soldiers sleep, he'd say. You'll never have backache that way. It was also a check that they weren't fiddling with themselves. You were never too young for sins of the flesh. There were other checks too. They learned to recite a prayer in the morning:

'Angel of God, my guardian dear,
To whom God's love commits me here,
Ever this day be at my side,
To light, to guard, to rule and guide.'

When they realised that this angel could also snoop on their most private conversations and actions they ceased to invoke him. Nobody likes squealers.

Immediately he left they would pull up their knees, replace their hands between their·thighs to warm them and resume the armchair position which allowed heat to be shared.

When Mr Toner went downstairs the master storyteller, Bern, would resume. He had the advantage of seeing more films; the obligatory retelling of these, much embellished, formed the substance of his tales. *Reap the Wild Wind* was a favourite, especially the part where the octopus grabs the diver in the sunken treasure ship, breaks his air line, strangles him, then drags him struggling down to his dark lair. Dominic would cover his ears for that part even when Bern said the diver was the bad guy and he had it coming to him. The chap always got the girl, except in *Geronimo* and *Custer's Last Stand*. When the younger ones eventually saw the films for themselves they were not nearly as entertaining.

The boys' room had two beds, a double for Bern and Joe, a single for Dominic, the youngest. Their two sisters slept in the small front room and the parents occupied the room in between. It would be years before they would dare trespass on that sacred territory with its black wooden bedside locker which contained only a pile of silvery badges in the image of doves, representing the Holy Ghost. Mr Toner was a member of some confraternity run by his priest cousin. He never got around to distributing the badges.

On winter mornings it was lovely to be wakened by the sound of the radio and know you didn't have to get up yet. Mr Toner was often due at work in the brewery at six o'clock, especially approaching Christmas. And little thanks I get for it, he used say. Nowadays they wouldn't recognise work if it jumped up and bit them.

Mr Toner made the porridge the previous night and had only to heat it up for his breakfast. While he shaved, the radio murmured the morning litany that would constitute part of the memory of most children living in the British Isles in that period: Lundy, Sole, Fastnet, Shannon, Malin, Iceland, Faroes, Dogger which Dominic thought was the Dodder, the river that flowed at the back of their garden. The names were indelibly imprinted on their memories and so was 'Lilliburlero', the tune that announced the news and which their father said the English had stolen from them.

The ritual never varied, six days a week, summer and winter. They waited for the radio to be switched off, the voice calling softly up the stairs, 'I'm off, Mam.' Then they heard the back door opening. There would be a pause while he collected his bike from the shed, then the creak of the side gate, the clatter of the front gate and they could go back to sleep until it was time for Mrs Toner to heat up the porridge for them. When he was first married their father owned an old Harley-Davidson motorcycle and a side car which he built himself and into which the first babies were crammed. They saw the photo of the machine in the glasscase and hoped he would get another, but he never did.

The Toners lived in a cul-de-sac of about eighty houses built in Council style by some socially aware townplanner in the thirties. He located the scheme in the middle of one of the poshest suburbs in Dublin. Whether the intention was to improve the manners of its working-class inhabitants or to apply a little Bolshevik jab to the local bourgeoisie it would be difficult to say. But lest there be squeals of protest – or possibly as a result of protests from the respectable residents – a facade

13

of ten or eleven more opulent houses was erected at the entrance to the ghetto. These effectively camouflaged the swarming little development. Delicate sensibilities, not to mention property values, were therefore protected. It suited the residents of the cul-de-sac too because they prided themselves on being house owners, not Council tenants. These were utility houses, built by a private developer and purchased on long-term mortgages.

The Toner family arrived in their grandfather's pony and cart in the year the Second World War started. They had escaped from the less desirable area of Drimnagh whose address automatically branded them as Council or Corporation dwellers. In those straitened days degrees of poverty were perceived more sharply than distinctions between rich and poor. Nothing changes.

Dominic was barely old enough to remember the excitement of the journey on a moonlit night, the cart crammed with children and the smaller household goods, their mother holding on to them for dear life while Granda Hope urged on their very own snow white steed with flowing mane called Kit, after Kit Carson of course, who in daylight was an undersized, overburdened, dirty-grey animal with sores on its knees. It had a long tail that whipped at their faces while their Granda cursed it, 'Will you hup outa that, you lazy streepach.'

On the short, steep hill down to the cul-de-sac, which would later be perfect for toboggans, they felt terror, sure that the pony would slip and they would go tumbling over its back. No such thing happened and they were greeted by Mr Toner and the older children who had earlier that day cycled across the south city suburbs of Harold's Cross and Rathgar to meet the furniture van. Dominic, already half asleep, went out like a light.

· TWO ·

THE NEW HOME WAS PARADISE, halfway between city and country. There were plenty of other kids and friendly neighbours. The river lined it on one side, squeezing the rows of terraced houses like toothpaste against the mini-escarpment of the Churchtown hill. Although this gave it a tucked-in character which Drimnagh could never have, it also made it the most unsalubrious location for miles around: a damp, low-lying area which caused the river to flood the houses down at the end every few winters. The nice people living in the surrounding areas nicknamed it Smokey Hollow because on summer mornings the settlement was shrouded in mist and in winter the smoke from coal fires gave the same effect. Fog always remained thickest over the Hollow. To the children, this gave it a magical dimension.

It also gave them the opportunity to get their own back on cranky neighbours. They would tie a long piece of thread to a door knocker, feed it out as delicately as a fuse, then, retreating towards the safety zone, tug sharply, hear the knocker rattling as the thread broke, destroying the evidence. It was thrilling simply to stand still and know they were invisible, to hear the screeched imprecations of the householder as he or she peered uselessly into the grey blanket.

The children familiarised themselves with the neighbours by means of a simple game played every night after lights out:
– Who lives in number sixty-one?
– The O'Briens.
– Wrong.
– The Murtaghs.
– Wrong.

– Give up.

– The Woodisons.

– What! They do not. They live in number sixty-three. I was there only yesterday.

– You're wrong.

– Wanna bet?

And so on until they fell asleep.

The first row the Toner kids had with their new neighbours was about who was going to play the devil in the play in Lynch's shed. It was really Joe's row but they were all dragged in because the previous night they had been regaled by Bern's version of *The Three Musketeers* in the Classic cinema.

– So, said Joe to Bern when the row broke out. One for all and all for one, right?

– Oh all right, said Bern grudgingly. There was no backing out even if Bern hadn't the faintest interest in play-acting and particularly in stupid plays about ghosts and devils.

Every play in Lynch's shed featured a ghost or a devil. It was the best thing about the plays. In fact it was the only substantial thing that happened. All plots were improvised and whether they were about nagging wives and drunkard husbands, policemen and robbers, mad professors who had sold their souls to the devil and were going to blow up the world – no matter, all led up to the point where the kid lucky enough to get the part draped himself in a sheet and leaped out from the wings bellowing at everybody that he was the devil or the ghost, whichever suited the narrative. This was the cue as well as the excuse for everybody to start shouting and roaring.

The key to the role was the sheet. Whoever could provide the costume automatically got the part. Mothers refused point-blank to lend such expensive items. They always got dirty and invariably got torn. If the sheets were newish it was out of the question. If they were old and patched the neighbours would know whose it was. So it had to be taken without permission and returned with nobody the wiser. Whoever had the nerve to do this deserved the part of the ghost/devil.

Joe, waiting in the wings as it were, was perceptive enough to see this as a shortcut to acceptance in the gang and airily declared it'd be no bother to get one. He was duly promised the part. But when the day of the performance came he turned up and glumly reported failure. The mothers' grapevine had heard about the play so the linen cupboards and hot presses were policed too tightly.

There was only one solution and Davy Lynch knew it. It was his shed and he was overall impresario, playwright and chief actor. With a black look at Joe he slinged up his garden path. They saw him disappear into the kitchen and waited despondently for the indignant sounds of refusal from Mrs Lynch.

When Davy appeared with the sheet in his hands everyone was very impressed. The day, and the play, were saved. That's when the row started.

– Good man yourself, said Joe. Let's see how it fits.

– Of course it fits, said Davy, draping it over his own head.

Joe took a deep breath.

– No messing now. You said I could be the devil.

Davy lifted the sheet to reveal his incredulous expression.

– Are you codding! I got the sheet. I'm the devil.

He dropped the sheet over his face again and uttered an experimental growl.

– Don't annoy me, said Joe patiently.

– And you don't annoy me, said the devil.

– I'm warning you, said Joe.

The devil waved his arms derisively and turned his back on Joe. What was a frustrated actor to do?

– You're only a little shit, Davy Lynch, muttered Joe and directed a kick at the devil's backside.

The devil yelped, turned and kicked back wildly. He caught Joe in the goolies. Joe yelled in pain, crumpled briefly, then straightened up and lashed out with his fist at the part of the sheet where Davy's nose should be, and was. It was a direct hit, evidenced by a red stain seeping through the sheet. The devil had a bloody nose. Joe ran for his life.

That wasn't the end of it. His fellow actors pushed Davy's

head back, placed a bit of tin at the back of his neck and eventually stopped the nosebleed. Then they discussed what to do. The sheet's condition could be blamed on Joe Toner and compensation could be worked out between mothers. Joe would certainly get a hiding. In the meantime ... the red stain on the sheet was fascinating. It would be a shame to waste it.

They decided the show must go on. But as the devil was sort of like Dracula and didn't have any blood in his veins – or so the Slag Kelly said – the sheet would be used to represent the ghost of a murdered man. The temptation of a real blood-stained sheet was irresistible.

Back in the safety of his own garden, five houses away, Joe brooded. He would never be let in, even to watch the show. But he knew that security at the shed always became lax once the play started. That's when he demanded Bern's cooperation and together they concocted a plan of revenge.

The local children crowded into the shed for the performance. They were a noisy, jostling, catcalling lot. Even babies were there, bawling before the thing started, before the ghost even came out to frighten them. They sat on planks placed on wooden boxes. Those in the front row passed the time by ducking their heads through the sacks which served as curtains and bobbing quickly back to avoid the vicious kicks from the cast within.

The play started. It was a complex plot which neither the audience nor the cast could understand because no lines were audible. But Davy, playing one of his many roles, swaggered convincingly across the ten feet of stage dragging at a stolen cigarette and it was clear he was the detective brought in by the worried-looking woman, Maisie McGee, in a superlative performance marred only by the calls to show them her knickers. Various characters made entrances and exits, looking here and there for stolen jewels and bumping repeatedly and violently into each other, because that got the laughs.

There were numerous fights and one stabbing when Davy had to stagger interminably all over the place, dying for a long time. Then there was an interval where Ginty Scully tried to sing 'The Moon Behind the Hill' and was boohed off the stage. A rumour started among the audience that there was no ghost at all, otherwise why would they bore people with Ginty Scully who hadn't a note in his head. They began to stamp their feet.

– Give us our money back, they chanted, which was unjust because very few of them had paid the entrance fee – a jamjar on which Davy hoped to collect the penny refund.

So the climax had to be advanced a little in the play. It was Davy's big moment to don the sheet. On the corrugated roof of the shed, Bern and Joe crouched. They could follow the action easily by listening to the din and peering through the holes left by long-rusted nails. At the precisely correct moment, as Davy was about to make his big entrance, they lit twisted bits of newspaper and pushed them through a gap in two layers of the corrugated iron, directly over the stage area.

These missiles contained pieces of nitrate film, obtained from Mr Toner's workshop. They were the most effective stinkbombs of all, as was instantly recognised by the experts in the audience below. Not only did the bombs stink foully, they produced a satisfying volume of smoke.

No previous ghost ever produced such pandemonium. Both the stage and the seating were wrecked – rather, reverted to their normal status of planks and barrels – in the ensuing melee. Babies even stopped crying and gazed in wonder at the entertainment. Miraculously nobody got more than normal abrasions and the only real casualty was Mrs Lynch's sheet which was trampled in the rush. It was later agreed that it was the best play ever, and everybody congratulated Joe and Bern on their daring.

They even congratulated Davy on his inspired stage direction and he had to pretend that it was all arranged, but privately he told Joe it would be over his dead body if Joe ever appeared on stage again.

– It's only for sissies anyway, muttered Joe, smug that he didn't have the job of bringing home a bloody as well as torn and dirty sheet.

It was a kind of initiation rite for Bern and Joe as well as their siblings. It showed that you didn't mess around with the Toners, and on that level they fitted with ease into the community.

Across the stepping stones at the back of Toners' was a field with a long avenue of young pine trees clearly designed for hide-and-seek. On hot summer nights it was used also by courting couples, mainly army privates from Portobello Barracks who brought their mots on the tram from Rathmines to Dartry and persuaded them to walk in the field. But this was Hollow territory. People intruded at their own risk, and were fair game for the older children who could evade or ignore the evening chorus of parents calling that it was time to go to bed. Hollow children knew every bush, every tree in the field, could slip like wraiths through the twilight, cupping their mouths to say 'woooo, wooo' or whistle in brilliant imitation of the Indians they saw in the Classic, all to terrify the mots and drive them closer into the embrace of the soldiers who, in all equity, should have paid them and, in a sense, did.

Because after the evening's sport of pestering the recumbent and oddly-moving shapes – Donal Barry, whose family came originally from the country, so he should know, said the mots were milking the soldiers, whatever that meant – the children would return in the morning to find the occasional coin. They sometimes also found a kind of balloon which wouldn't blow up and which was greeted with horror by their mothers: 'Throw that dirty thing in the fire. I hope you didn't put it in your mouth.'

They shared the river with fishermen, courting couples and the occasional dead dog that floated down from Rathfarnham. It was superb for swimming. There was a bridge from which they could dive and a waterfall under whose sheet of falling light they could sidle and imagine themselves as Tarzan. Its banks provided shelter for bands of Robin Hoods, Jesse Jameses and Apaches who used the long stalks of wild rhubarb to repel townie gangs.

A mile away, Pogue's Valley was overflowing with blackberries, an asset to the permanently hungry kids. It was also on the route home from Saturday afternoon matinees in the Classic in Terenure. Then it became Death Valley to accommodate all the miniature cowboys and Indians who galloped through it, slapping their own backsides like the cowboys did when they were chasing stagecoaches or getting away from the posse.

There were convenient orchards for 'boxing the fox', places to keep out of sight when mitching from school and a sewage pipe which could be thrillingly penetrated in summer with the light from stolen boxes of matches. There was a row of six trees opposite their back window, one of which, as their father pointed out, contained a gorilla in its branches, who stayed motionless and menacing from a distance but always vanished when they climbed the tree!

To traverse this row of trees without touching ground was the initiation rite into the various gangs. If girls wanted to join they had to prove they'd done the task by leaving a miraculous medal on the top of the ultimate and most difficult tree. Mrs Toner got fed up supplying them with the medals. She also got fed up with the girls asking her to make shorts for them – not slacks which were considered 'fast' – so that they could climb the trees without those brats of boys looking up at their knickers. Few girls ever fulfilled all the conditions, which was just as well because their presence inhibited the boys when they wanted to recite the latest ditty:

'There was an old lady, God bless her,
Who threw her leg over the dresser.
The dresser was sticky,
And stuck to her mickey,
And no one could dress her, the messer.'

Once a foolish visitor from the country, a cousin of the Houghtons, attempted it and fell fifteen feet. He was lucky the barbed wire below broke his fall. He bounced safely, screeched that he had been pushed by the next initiate but couldn't prove it and was judged to be not the right material for the gang – a crybabby as well as a culchie. The child brought an interesting scar home to Clare.

Halfway down the cul-de-sac itself there was the Circle, a roundabout which was a kind of village green without grass. It was perfect for rounders (a kind of baseball), and cricket played with a hurley stick. Once the Council tried to sabotage these games by planting a shrub in the centre. It survived one unhappy season. The circumference of the Circle was the race track. One wonderful August during the war a man from Belfast brought his two children to visit their cousins in number forty-five. He was very rich and organised races with cash prizes of pennies and tuppences. There were also many consolation prizes of a farthing, the coin with the kingfisher which was pretty but could buy only two aniseed sweets, better known as Nancyballs.

The children felt sorry for the visitors not winning any of the races but, after all, the strangers had full-time access to a rich father, whom they addressed musically as 'Dohray', presumably Belfastese for Daddy. One of the children tried this name out on Mr Toner, in the hope that it might loosen his purse strings too, but all he got was a quare look, a ruffle of the newspaper and a shake of the head that said: Blessed God, am I rearing imbeciles as well!

· THREE ·

THE DWELLERS IN SMOKEY HOLLOW WERE A MIXTURE of labourers, craftsmen, clerks, postmen, Catholics, Protestants. There were five policemen, one of whom had served in Palestine and two who played brass instruments in the police band. There was a German shoemaker who wore wellingtons all the time so they thought he must be a spy and they called him Funf, like the character in Tommy Hanley's programme on the radio, ITMA. Funf was a poor spy because he never learned fluent English and he was mocked pitilessly, not only by the children, but by his wife too. Perhaps his English was so limited that he did not even understand his wife's insults because when she died in bed he barricaded the house. It took the authorities three days to collect the corpse.

An unmarried brother and sister lived together at the top of the road and had pockmarked faces whose cause was darkly rumoured to be a social disease. There was a boy with six toes who was the envy of the other kids. There was a couple of tramway men, one of them an inspector who had the best garden in the Hollow. There was the inevitable Corkman – he came with a one-way ticket to Dublin – who said 'Deeah git' (Gaelic for 'God be with you') to everybody and was pitied. There were two alcoholics, both very gentle and one of whom always spoke in refined tones to himself as he wended his way home. There was a frail music teacher living at the back of the Dodder who was called Oul' Theory. She used a knitting needle as a sort of metronome cum blunt instrument to beat time into unruly fingers. She greeted her pupils at the door with rosary beads twined in her fingers which supported the rumour that she was a nun on holidays.

23

There was a family from Mayo who never lost their accent or lifestyle. They didn't bother with a shed for their turf but built a professional-looking rick in their tiny back garden. This still left room to grow potatoes. There was even an atheist, a rough man with a big lorry under which he spent most of his time working. He had a sign made to hang over his porch. The porch was pretentious enough; it didn't come with the house. To have a sign was really getting above one's station. But the name on it, St Cloud, was said by some to be just made up because they had never heard of such a saint and he probably did it to insult his deeply religious neighbours. The Toners were unfortunate enough to live beside him.

The work ethic dominated. Every husband had a job; every wife worked in the house. The only self-employed person was Mr Coyne who had a hackney cab. Later one of the policeman started a mattress-teasing business and put an ad in the paper saying 'our vans' would collect and deliver anywhere. He was the first entrepreneur in the Hollow. Every time his ancient, battered red van passed, the kids would screech out 'our vans' in mocking tones. They were articulating their elders' attitude to any kind of pretension, people getting above themselves. It was a tight little community.

Mr Toner was a cooper employed by the firm of Arthur Guinness at St James's Gate. He was good at mending bicycles, growing vegetables and repairing the house. But because he also sang, painted pictures and went on about art and beauty, some of his children were uncertain about how he should be described. He wrote long poems about nature and God in a perfect copperplate hand. His writing was so clear that he could turn the page on its side and cover it with a further layer of words which would also be legible, a trick he said he had learned from his grand aunt who liked to save paper.

Even when he painted and varnished the front door he used three kinds of comb, made of wood, rubber and tin, to put a realistic grain in the paint. He could simulate knots, too, which looked like the real thing and prompted Joe to ask why did he bother painting it at all, why didn't he just leave the original wood, knots and all? Mr Toner just gave Joe one of them looks.

He sang while working and said Caruso was the greatest tenor who ever lived but that he overdid it and his heart burst when he was giving a concert in a hall. They looked around their tiny hallway. They imagined a bloody mess on the walls.

In school the nun asked the children about their respective fathers' occupations. It was Dominic's bad luck that she should pick on him first.

– He's an em ... he's an em ...

– Yes, Dominic?

– He's an artist, sister.

– An artist?

She beamed knowingly at the rest of the class.

– And what does your father the artist do, Dominic?

– Em. Sister, em, he fixes the bikes and everything and ... I dunno.

– You don't know. Well now, Dominic, listen to me. And you too, children. We mustn't tell lies about our parents. They are hard-working people. What is the fourth commandment? Honour thy ...? father and ...? thy mother. Very good. Now, Dominic, your father has a job, hasn't he?

– Yes, sister.

– He works hard, doesn't he?

– Yes, sister.

– So he is a working man?

– I think so, sister.

– Well. Jesus was the son of a working man and he wasn't ashamed to say so, was he?

– No, sister.

– Artist, indeed. And you named after the order of preachers, men who saved the Church.

Whatever that meant, Dominic seethed with shame and embarrassment, not because he had met his first sadist but because Lanky Treacy was smirking. He whispered, 'I'll get you after.' Lanky sniffed.

On the way home the other fellows insisted he carry out his threat. He didn't want to fight Lanky who was, after all, a neighbour, but the peer pressure was too much. Lanky's height made him ungainly. He also had the psychological disadvantage of being forced to take piano lessons.

He was no scrapper but he had guts. When Canon Roy, who owned the school, came in to the class and asked which was the best football team in the country, Lanky said 'Cavan' because that's where his father came from. But the Canon came from Kerry so he wasn't taking any nonsense. He gave Lanky a slap every time he got the Cavan answer. This went on for a while but Lanky didn't give in, even when everybody could see he was nearly bawling. Later Cavan beat Kerry in the Polo Grounds in New York which might have been the real cause of Lanky's smirk.

There was a quarry in Rathgar which was bottomless. They knew this because the Corporation had been trying without success to fill it in for years. Drowned people floated to the surface and moaned at twilight. Millions of people had heard them, Ginty Scully said, so that was the time to avoid it. But during the day it was harmless enough and was used as a venue for bloodletting and duels. On the banks of the quarry Dominic easily wrestled Lanky to the ground and then lost interest. Lanky rose like a giraffe, adopted a boxing pose and said:

– I'll burst you.

He dared Dominic to attack. But the only reason for continuing was to save Lanky's pride and Dominic had other things on his mind, like what the hell his father really was. He turned his back, picked up his schoolbag and headed home, followed at a dignified distance by Lanky. The others jeered them both in frustration.

– Cowardy, cowardy custard, stick your head in mustard.
– Go home and tell your oulwan.
– Eh, Lanky, is it cold up there?
– Dommo, you're not worth a shit. You should have got him, the long streak of misery.

Dominic wondered who was more to blame, the nun or his father. He saved the question for the next time he saw his father painting.

– What's an artist, Da?

– It's somebody who uses his talent to praise his creator.

– How?

– By painting pictures or making sculptures.

– Are you one?

– One what?

– You draw pictures. Are you an artist?

His father frowned over a line, tilting his head back and squinting under his spectacles to get the right perspective.

– I'm just a doodler. Art is a God-given talent. Real artists spend all their time at it.

– So you're not?

– Not what?

– An artist.

His father suspended his concentration to consider the small nuisance interrogating him. He made an effort.

– Maybe I'm a quare artist.

– What's a quare artist?

– Would you not be annoying me with your questions. I'm trying to get this right before the light fades. Go out yourself and play while there's still daylight.

Dominic turned away in disgust. The nun was right. Besides, how could anybody be an artist who ate a boiled egg like his father: beating it round the top with an inverted spoon, scooping the lid off carefully, tapping salt on it and then because it was hot sucking it in with his breath and a horrible slurping noise. It was the ugliest sound in the world, worse even than Mr Ryan up the top of the road coughing his lungs out in the morning as they passed on their way to school.

Some people can't tell their art from their elbow, Mr Toner used to say. Like that crowd in the Academy. They think you're not an artist unless you speak in a toney accent. You'd think they'd marbles in their mouth. Well, I won't change my accent for the likes of them.

Mrs Toner urged him to try it once, to submit his pictures to the Academy.

– I'll submit them to nobody, he said. Anyway, I'd suffocate in the middle of them West Brit accents. We didn't burn enough of them out in 1920.

Mrs Toner wrapped up two of the big pictures in brown paper and with the help of Bern lugged them on the bus down to Kildare Street. She reported back that evening.

– Well, you were right, she said. A young pup with a fancy accent looked at me as if I had two heads. 'Is your husband a member of the Academy,' he said, and him with a sneer on his face. I nearly threw the pictures at him.

– What did I tell you! They're all the same.

– Well, at least he took them in. He said the judges would have a look at them. And if they were accepted you'd get an invitation to varnishing day.

– Judges, my ah. All they know is modern rubbish, daubs and squiggles. Look at Picasso. They hang his pictures baw-ways and nobody knows the difference. Chancers that can't even draw a straight line.

As it happened, most of the exhibition consisted of pretty pictures exactly like Mr Toner's. His pictures were turned down, of course, and it took Mrs Toner months to retrieve them from the dusty basement in Kildare Street. He never allowed her to try again. 'I have my pride,' he said.

Nevertheless it was undeniable that the pictures he drew of the kids were as good as photographs. Maybe that's why he did it. Photos were expensive. But he took plenty of them too, so there must be some difference. Even the pictures he painted of the two waterfalls on the Dodder looked real, except when you passed the real thing on miserable winter days and there were neither sleepy cows on the banks nor leaves on the trees.

Mr Toner would sometimes go out on his bike early on Sunday morning with the black wooden paintbox which he had designed to fit under the crossbar, a waterproof coat tied to the handlebars and another box strapped on the back carrier.

He would not return until evening, having cycled to Glen-dalough, forty miles away, spent the day drawing and painting and cycled home again in the evening. He used to boast that he got there as fast as the bunch of youngsters on racing bikes who would whiz past him as he plodded along. The reason was that they would stop regularly for breaks and he would overtake them.

These things were remembered by children trying desperately to see something to boast about in this untypical father. All right, he said he had once nearly stowed away with an English pal of his on a Norwegian schooner down at the Dublin docks. He even remembered the name of the schooner, *The Twickenham*, which didn't sound Norwegian, so maybe he was making the whole thing up.

But he didn't actually do it, so what good was talking about it? He'd never been in a typhoon around Cape Horn like all the heroes in the books. Okay, he intended to – so what! He was always saying that hell was paved with good intentions. Wasn't that what he was doing himself? What's the good of saying you nearly might have if you didn't?

You wouldn't talk like that to him, though. If, like Bern, you politely queried some of his claims, you'd be told you don't understand, wait until you're older. That's if you were lucky. More likely you'd get a clip on the ear.

He also wanted to be buried in Glendalough, between the round tower and the lakes. His children would never fulfil this request.

While he sketched, shaved himself or mended shoes he sang: 'On with the Motley', 'Friend of Mine', 'Nirvana', 'Love Could I Only Tell Thee' and 'Annie Dear'. Annie was his wife's name, although he always called her Nan or Mam. She could sing too, but only on special occasions. Then the pair of them would render 'The Moon Hath Raised' from *The Lily of Killarney*, him urging her to be brave at the last fence, the four high ascending notes at the end: My ... heart's ... de ... light. They had learned it when they were courting and performed it on very special occasions.

The children enjoyed it when he was mending their shoes and singing 'The Cobbler's Song' from *Chu Chin Chow*:

'The better my work, the less I earn,
For the soles ne'er crack nor the uppers turn.'

Then he would hold a battered shoe up and complain. 'That

man didn't have kids like me. How in God's name do you wear them out? Look at the heels! What way do you walk at all? If I catch you playing football in these ... '

He used the round piano stool as a bench and held the three-footed cobbler's last between his knees. It reminded them of the Isle of Man where Mr and Mrs Toner had spent their honeymoon and the proof was an ashtray in the glasscase with the same running legs. He would carefully mark the shape of the sole on the new rectangle of white leather, place the pencil behind his ears, reach for the knife: 'Where did I put it? I can leave nothing down. Didn't I tell you not to fiddle with that!', and cut the new sole out cleanly. Their job was to bring it out to the sink and place it in the two inches of water, then retrieve it when he called for it. Then he would beat hell out of it with the hammer before tacking it on. Even with his mouth full of tacks he would continue singing.

'For prince and cobbler, poor and rich,
Stand in need of a cobbler's stitch.
Why then worry what lies before,
Hangs this life by a thread no more.'

It sounded cheerful but try as he might when he grew up Dominic could never remember them laughing heartily. His father occasionally showed a wispy sort of smile to visitors and his mother could sometimes be seen with her hand to her mouth as if she was concealing a giggle. But maybe this was only from the time half of her jawbone was cut away because of the cancer and she always had her hand to her face, and created a hat whose veil cunningly concealed the unsightly absence. No, that was much later. Time mixes up memories.

· FOUR ·

ON SATURDAYS ONE BOTTLE OF STOUT WAS PROVIDED for Granda Hope. He had skin like a walnut, all crinkly and brown. His fingers were knobbly from working outdoors all his life and he had a hearty voice. He kept pigs for a living in the back garden of his terraced cottage in Churchtown. The street was called Moran's Avenue, after the oldest resident, Jimmy Moran, also a pig breeder and Granda Hope's nextdoor neighbour. Between the two of them on summer days the odour was stupendous. When hygiene regulations later put an end to this industry and death put an end to the two old men the Corporation changed the name of the road to Beauville Avenue in keeping with the new residential desirability of the area.

Granda Hope collected what they called 'the feeding' – slop or pig swill – from the local area and Saturday was his day for Smokey Hollow. It was also his day for gossiping with his daughter and enjoying his grandchildren.

As he sat and sipped his Guinness one or other of the three brothers would take his turn to do the rounds with the odoriferous pony and cart. The smell was awful. The job was humiliating. If it had been for anybody else but Granda Hope they might have objected – a big might. First of all, on what grounds could they object? That it was socially demeaning? That would have been a slight on their Granda, whom they wouldn't hurt for all the world. Secondly, in that household you didn't object too loudly to jobs. You'd either get a clatter or an interminable lecture about parents working their fingers to the bone for ungrateful wretches who didn't know how lucky they were having a good home and three meals a day and so on. They suspected Mr Toner didn't approve too much

of his sons being turned into slop gatherers, but whether it was
for peace sake or because he thought it would teach them that
life was real and life was earnest – for whatever reason, he said
nothing.

The only escape tactic might be to make yourself scarce
before Granda arrived, but that would mean missing a part of
the omnibus edition of 'Dick Barton Special Agent'. It wasn't
worth such a sacrifice. Dutifully they submitted to the weekly
chore.

If, as sometimes happened, they had to collect from the
house of a young one whom they currently fancied, the only
thing to do was whistle brazenly and adopt the demeanour of
a working man in the hope that she'd think you were all grown up.

Sometimes, for gas, to take a rise out of them, or because
there was nothing better to do, their own pals would call after
them, 'Slop, slop, the pigs is dyin'.' Pal or no pal, you didn't
joke about things like that. It was a delicate enough balance to
keep your dignity while you heaved buckets of their leavings
into the back of the cart. It could and did lead to bloody noses
as the brother on duty lost his temper at the insult. The only
one who enjoyed the tension was Kit the pony, who would
stray away from the battle and feed on the succulent hedges,
which caused more screeching from neighbours.

When Dominic was old enough to take his turn, the first
thing he did was misjudge the gap between the cart and Mr
Coyne's hackney cab. He crushed in the front wing of the cab.
After that his grandfather accompanied him for a while.

On Friday evenings they would run up to the top of the
Hollow to see their grandparents passing on their way home
to Churchtown: their Granny a bulky black silhouette hugging
her shopping and the residual warmth of a ball of malt taken
in Murphys of Rathgar. Their Granda, fortified by his bottle of
stout, was Ben Hur, all flailing arms and cries to Kit the pony
to 'hup owa that'. But Kit knew the road so well that she needed
little encouragement to gather impetus going down the Orwell
Hill in preparation for the ascent of Churchtown Hill. On the
flat section between hills at the top of the Hollow she would

be going like a rocket, her shoes striking sparks from the road.

The pony's liveliness was actually a hazard for Granda Hope. When he was leaving any place she would hardly wait for him to heave himself up into his seat before she accelerated. This was all right until his bones began to stiffen up. One day outside Toners' he was too slow and she moved while he was in mid-ascent. His foot slipped off the iron step and he fell to the ground while Kit went zooming away. What awed the children was that he held on to the reins even while he was being dragged along the road round the Circle. He reminded them of the hero in the pictures stopping the runaway stage with the mot inside, although in their worldliness they decided he was just hanging on for dear life to the only means of livelihood he possessed.

Eventually, outside number forty, the headstrong pony realised something was wrong and stopped, but not before her master was badly bruised. In fact there was no little heroism in the deed. He was afraid of the havoc a runaway pony and cart might wreak in a street full of playing children. They realised this as he tried to get a word in edgeways while Mrs Toner bathed his wounds and gave out to him for being such an obstinate man in not taking people's advice and getting rid of that pony which would be the death of somebody – and don't say I didn't warn you!

While the old man was recovering, Dominic was let off school to help him do the rounds of the area. In Orwell Park he was collecting slop from a big house when an elderly man came out to greet his grandfather and thank him for returning a spoon he had found in the offal. He looked at Dominic carefully.

– It's not many youngsters nowadays would do this job, he said, even to help their grandfather.

This momentarily pleased Dominic until he realised the implication that there must be some kind of stigma attached to the job. After that he was very self-conscious about it.

The sores on the pony's knees seemed to be a permanent fixture and Granda Hope was dismissive of them. Eventually somebody reported him to the SPCA and Kit was put down. It was a serious loss. Granda Hope had to borrow Oul' Jimmy Moran's pony for his rounds which was a terrible ignominy as they were, in a sense, in friendly competition for pig feeding. Part of every Saturday was devoted to reminiscence about Kit and a furious tirade against the busybody who had reported him.

– An oul' bitch with little to do but spy.

– How do you know it was a woman?

– Men understand these things. Only a woman would interfere. I've had ponies all my life and them sores would have cleared up themselves.

– When?

– In God's good time.

His daughter nodded doubtfully. The children took their cue from her.

– Did the sores hurt?

– What! Ponies are not whinging little crybabbies. That pony was like a child to me. Would I let her be hurt! Wouldn't she let me know if she was hurting?

– If she couldn't cry how would you know she was hurting?

Granda Hope gave knowing nods.

– That pony could tell you the day that was in it. Doesn't she know every house on the round? Ponies can let you know things.

A deep slurp from his glass.

– Ponies know more than rips that have nothing better to do than to be going around spying on people.

Granda Hope was their favourite relation. He was open and innocent, brash and good-humoured, a contrast and relief to the complication that was their father. Granda Hope never wore gloves, not even when it was snowing, although he would stamp his feet, blow on his hands and roar, 'Damn the weather!' He greatly approved of the children and when surrounded by them would laugh and declare, 'I love them childher.' They noticed that their father was always reserved in the old man's presence, as if he didn't really approve of such garrulousness.

The old man was quieter in his own home, a small house with a trellis porch on which wild woodbine grew in summer. Here, Granny Hope was the boss. She kept chickens, made marmalade and fell asleep listening to the radio. The living room was cluttered with pictures – 'The Angelus', 'The Potato Pickers', 'Love's Young Dream', a photo of the uncle after whom Dominic was named, the crucifix made from bullets, the tasselled cloth on the high mantelpiece, the black horsehair settee, their own parents' wedding photo. Mrs Toner looked like a gypsy, dark and with luminous eyes. They loved being there except when their Granny hawked and dropped a big gollyer in the spittoon beside her chair.

Granda mixed the pig feed in huge vats in the yard, boiling it before he gave it to the screeching pigs. The baby bonhams were pink and lovable but their mother was ugly. Once the children came too close and the big sow chased Joe up the yard. He never lived it down because Granny Hope chortled that he was carrying a yard brush and could have given it a belt on the snout. That would have put a stop to its gallop, I'm telling you.

Granda's dog was a big, sleepy, white and brown collie named Tom and it lazed in the sunshine all day, yawning at intervals. It confused Dominic because there was an uncle by the same name. So the two personalities merged into a hairy humanoid. He gave the dog a wide berth because when it yawned he expected a man's voice to come out. At least that's what happened in his nightmares. It also snapped at thin air and they thought it was imitating the lion at the start of the films until Granda said it was only eating flies, of which there were swarms because of the pigs.

– What use is he? they asked.
– He keeps the rats down, Granda Hope said.
– Rats?
– As big as a house.
– What about the cats?
– Cats is only out for themselves.

Granny Hope made marmalade and when she was in a good mood called to them in the yard through the kitchen window and smiled a smile they would always remember. The kitchen was a kind of temporary outhouse covered in tar which made a terrific noise when it rained. But the living room, the only other room they were allowed into, was solid and quiet and comforting. She had a much bigger radio than the Toners. But she wouldn't let them touch it because she said every time that little tyke, Bern, came near it he banjaxed it and Mr Toner had to come up and fix it. Mr Toner was good at things like that, although he said the radio was an antique, on its last legs, and she just used Bern as an excuse to make him trudge all the way up there to do other jobs.

– Oh, and by the way, while you're here, would you have a look at the Sacred Heart light and the electric iron? I wouldn't trust that oul' fool with this electricity.

– When I win the Sweep, Mr Toner would say, I'll buy her a new radio and that'll put an end to it.

The radio would have been a serious loss because she used it to fall asleep to after her dinner every day. Her favourite programme was 'Worker's Playtime' on the BBC with Emilio Macari and his accordion band which was guaranteed to put her to sleep. She also liked 'Housewives' Choice' in the morning, she said, and when the compere joined in the signature tune at the end, so did she: '... see you all again tomorrow morning, da-da-da-da.'

Apart from being fond of her, the children were in awe of her friendship with the manager of the Green cinema. Every Sunday afternoon she got the bus into town for the matinee and this man wouldn't let her queue but provided her with a seat in the foyer until the doors opened. Then he let her in for nothing. But once, when she brought her grandchildren with her, they were appalled to find that she fell asleep after ten minutes and snored through the whole film. What a waste. They tried to waken her but she brushed them off irritably. Old people are ridiculous.

She refused pointblank to bring Granda with her because the one time she did relent he and his buddy, Oul' Jimmy Moran, made a show of her at a critical point in a Humphrey

Bogart film. The crook was going to stab Bogart from behind and Oul' Jimmy shouted out, 'Be Christ, look out or he'll kill you', and the whole cinema convulsed and Granny Hope woke up to see everybody laughing at her. The shame of it, she said. Never again.

At home every evening in winter at a quarter to seven the kids tuned in to 'Dick Barton Special Agent'. Dick, Jock and Snowy were the chaps, the heroes. They could reproduce the dialogue.

– Sacramento doononares, the villian would say, and Dick would say, Get him, Snowy.

– Right, Guv, said Snowy.

Crunch.

– Oh, you blighter, that's not playing the game.

Ugh.

– Get him, Jock.

Thud.

– Try that, would you.

Aargh.

– He's getting away.

The funny thing was they never used any curses. Well, you wouldn't expect Dick Barton to say anything. He was the boss and sort of wellbred like all heroes. But nobody, not even the crooks, said Jasus or feck it or anything, even when they were getting clattered. Still, they all lived in London or somewhere, where everybody spoke proper.

After Dick Barton they turned to the sponsored pro-grammes on Radio Luxembourg. The best was the Penguins. They hadn't the faintest idea what was being advertised. They just liked the tune: 'We're marching along with a smile and a song, Oh it's fun to be one of the Penguins. We're loyal and true in whatever we do, Oh it's fun to be one of the Penguins.' They didn't even know what the Penguins were supposed to be. Some kind of club, or something. Nor did they care.

Then there was the one where the chorus was: 'Silvikrin puts the Ooh in shampoo' but the mot who sang it didn't wait for the same amount of beats to repeat the chorus. They supposed the advertisement cost money to broadcast and she was just saving time. But it was irritating, especially to Dominic, who liked songs to behave properly.

Saturday was dreary because Mr Toner insisted on listening to 'Making and Mending', on Radio Éireann, which was about laying lino and making lazy beds and rubbish like that. There was also a programme of *céilí* music where they heard a fellow called Rory O'Connor step-dancing and at the end one night the announcer said, 'You have been listening to' etcetera and then paused and said what sounded like: 'And that's your fucking lot.' They looked at each other. Were they hearing things? They looked at their parents to see the shock on their faces. Mr Toner rustled his paper loudly and said nothing. Not a word. They made sure to listen again the following week to see what the man actually said but it was a different announcer so they never knew.

One of their main favourites was Arthur Askey on the BBC who called out, 'Hello playmates', and sang a song about a bee: 'Oh what a glorious thing to be, a little busy, busy, busy bee.' There was also a song that stuck in their minds: 'We three, in Happidrome, working for the BBC, Ramsbottom and Enoch and Me.' And there was Wilfrid Pickles and 'Give 'im the Money, Barney', until Barney died and a woman named Mabel gave it out.

They used get *Radio Fun* and the *Knockout* to see their stars in cartoon form. They also swapped comics with other kids, so for each one they bought they could read about ten others.

The worst time for radio was on Mondays at lunch hour. It was awful. There was not only the remainder of the Sunday joint to be eaten cold but there was a sponsored programme on Radio Éireann with a tenor named Christopher Something who sang Irish ballads flat. Irish tenors were the vogue. Anybody that sounded like John McCormack was in. The funny thing, as Mr Toner kept on saying, was that they were all imitating the recordings of Irish ballads which McCormack made at the end of his career when his voice was gone, so they were imitating a has-been: scooped notes, short breath, country accent and all. That's why they sounded so terrible and why Christopher Something could get away with it.

– All chancers, said Mr Toner. I bet none of them would try 'Il Mio Tesoro'. That's the real test of a tenor. Look at what McCormack does in the middle with perfect breath control. What a singer. We only hear imitations nowadays.

They decided he must be jealous because he was a baritone. Still, he used to insist on silence when Radio Éireann played McCormack singing 'I Hear You Calling Me'. That was all right. Even the kids liked that. The only McCormack imitator Mr Toner would tolerate was a Scotsman named Fr Sidney McEwan who sang 'Oh, Mary we crown thee with blossoms today …' and other holy garbage. But the kids felt their father's tolerance was encouraged less by the man's musical ability than the fact that he was a priest. Nobody would criticise a priest. It was just as well because Fr Sidney was made into a canon.

The only serious competition that the BBC had in this household was the Sunday play on Radio Éireann, and that, fortunately, was immediately after 'Grand Hotel' with Albert Sandler and the Palm Court Orchestra. 'Ladies and Gentlemen, welcome to Grand Hotel. Straight through the glass doors …'

'Crash,' Joe would mutter and Mr Toner would scrunch his lips, ask was it impossible to get a bit of peace in this house and then settle down to hum along, move his lips with or give a scornful critique of the pieces and songs that he knew by heart. English baritones all have a wobble he would say, definitively. But that Gwen Catley is a real soprano. You'd think she was a real swallow singing. She's nearly as good as Galli Curci. The Sunday play was sacred. Even on summer evenings, after or before their walk with Mr Toner, they all looked forward to sitting down and listening to this treat. *The Monkey's Paw* terrified them out of their wits. Mrs Toner wept at *A Son a Priest* and looked speculatively at her male offspring. There was a play called *A Fantasia* in which the Irish language was outlawed and all the oulwans in Moore Street started speaking it for spite: *'Pingin an cabáiste'*. As Mr Toner said, 'The only way they'll revive the language is to forbid the Irish to speak it.'

Neither parent had learned Irish in school – Joe used to say they didn't know how lucky they were – but Mr Toner felt it his duty to encourage the use of Our Native Tongue. So he would say, *'Dún an doras'* and Joe would mutter, *'Tá mé i mahogany gaspipe*; shut the door wide open.' Mr Toner was also trying to learn Italian – for his singing – and French – because his ambition was to bring his wife to Lourdes for whatever ailed her – and he sometimes got them mixed up. *'Passez vous an siúcre, per favor,'* he might say, to the derision of his children. Maybe he was just codding, though.

Then there was 'Question Time' with Joe Linnane whom they thought was too smart for his own good. He's inclined to be smutty too, reproved Mrs Toner. But they had to admit he was talented. He could play the musical clues on the piano very well and as piano playing was the greatest social asset, the compere couldn't be dismissed completely.

'The Foley Family' they could identify with. Mr Foley was a pompous old fool, but funny. It was only when they heard the same actor's easily identifiable voice being used in other plays that they lost interest.

When Dominic was four his mother abandoned him. They told him she was just gone into hospital for a short while but he knew they were lying. She was gone forever and he cried at night under the covers for fear she was dead somewhere. It didn't seem to bother the others, as far as he could tell. Laura took over the housekeeping and their father stopped working overtime so that he was home early every evening. He would take Dominic on his knee and make a stuffed, moth-eaten dog talk to him. That wasn't bad. Mr Toner even did his famous Egyptian dance, where his head slid backwards and forwards on his shoulders and his hands pointed in peculiar directions. He sang his song about Susanna the Funniful Man, which involved snorting, grunting and whistling in quick succession and which had them in hysterics. It was difficult to reconcile this comic man with their serious day-to-day father.

When they told him his mother was due back the following

day Dominic wouldn't believe them. All day he waited impatiently, returning every five minutes to the front window to peer out through the net curtain so that he wouldn't miss her first appearance at the gate.

He spent a lot of time at this window, watching older children leaving for school and waiting for them to return, wondering would Emmett Dalton remember to cut out Mandrake the Magician for him from the *Evening Mail*. The Toners got the *Irish Press*. The reason Mandrake the Magician fascinated him was because all the characters in the comic strip had a single line on their cheeks which magically gave them high cheekbones. Maybe they were all related, even the crooks at whom Mandrake gestured hypnotically and Lothar, the big grey negro in the leopard skin who sometimes had to rescue Mandrake. Even Narda, Mandrake's mot, had it. Then there was a woman with a bun in her hair like Granny Hope who also had the line on her cheek and was a baddie who made him nervous.

If Emmett didn't bring the strip on the way to school Dominic would spend some time glancing through the *Book of Knowledge*, volume A to D, studying the black women with nothing on and babies dangling from their diddies. When Mr Toner noticed later how well-fingered they were, he removed the corrupting pages. He also did this with the pictures from Milton's *Paradise Lost* because the people falling down to hell had no clothes on either. And the top of the bookcase had glass doors which were locked to stop them reading *The Blue Lagoon* which was a famous dirty book.

In the late afternoon Mr Coyne's taxicab drew up outside and the unmistakeable black shape of his Granny emerged, followed slowly by his mother. She was carrying a white bundle very carefully. For some reason Dominic did not rush to the front door. He was mesmerised by the white bundle because he saw it move.

That's how he found out he was the baby no more.

· FIVE ·

THE BABY WAS CALLED YOUNG JOHNNY and was an awful nuisance. Of course the girls were mad about him and squabbled over whose turn it was to hold him and goohed and gahed over him and it would make you sick. You couldn't even touch him without Mrs Toner yelping about dirty hands, and they never saw such a waste as a shiny new four-wheeled vehicle, the pram, being thrown away on a kid that couldn't even explore its possibilities. It would have been perfect for going down the big hill, or crashing through enemy gangs, or even scutting. No, all such practical uses were barred with the familiar incantations: 'Mind the baby' or 'Do you want to kill the child?' or 'Wash your hands first' or 'If you do that once more!'

They could hardly move in the house without being told they'd wake the infant. My God, what would it be like if she'd had the two she claimed to have lost before this one? Anyway how could you lose a baby? No matter where you left it, its shrieks would attract attention. Not that such dark thoughts didn't occur to Dominic, who from a privileged position as the youngest had been catapulted out to fight his corner in the jungle of equality with his other siblings.

As if things weren't tough enough, there was the war. Wartime was when parents had the same frustrating response to every need: 'Do you not know there's a war on?' It was the perfect rejoinder whenever somebody wanted another piece of bread at teatime, or jam on their fourth slice, having already got their ration of jam on the third.

If they had ever seen a banana or orange other than in the cinema the memory of such luxuries was dim. Never having become accustomed to luxury they did not miss it although their stomachs often complained. The war itself, which the government called 'The Emergency' for some reason best known to themselves, was equally remote. It impinged on them only through comic cuts and the occasional aeroplane soaring miles above which the children all rushed out to see, crying 'Hail' Hitler. They all got gas masks which were tried on once, frightened the baby, and dumped on top of the wardrobe to gather dust until the mangy government repossessed them.

They were not so unaware that they did not sing with gusto the well-known ballad:

'Hitler had only got one ball
Goering had two but they were small
Himmler was something similar
But poor old Goebbels had no balls at all.'

They saw other fathers playing soldiers up at the bridge in the Local Defence Force commanded by Mr O'Toole, across the road. Although he was only a shoe salesman and meekly cleaned and polished his two sons' shoes every Saturday night, he never lost the martinet manner he developed in these few glorious years. It was interesting to see him rattling out orders to grown men, as if they were kids. The children of the neighbourhood had great gas yelling 'Ireland's Only Hope' after these patriots. The Toner children were uncertain whether to be glad or sorry that their own father, for whatever reason, was not one of them.

Real hardship never touched the family thanks to their father's steady job and their mother's unremitting labour. But you could not have persuaded the kids themselves that life was soft; because of a rigid work ethic which seemed to owe more to Calvinism than Catholicism they had to do their share too.

The Saturday round with the slop cart ensured nobody got ideas above their station. There was, besides, a full schedule of chores which included weeding the garden, trimming the hedge, getting coal, collecting cinders and running to Rathgar for messages. They all participated with varying degrees of resentment and efficiency in the washing up rota. The trick of breaking cups to prove oneself too awkward to be entrusted with the job lasted no time. Competence returned immediately they were deprived of their penny-a-week pocket money.

– If you're not able to wash up without breaking everything in sight then you're not fit to handle hard-earned money. And if you do it again you'll feel the back of my hand.

To the objection that other children on the road never washed up there was an impatient snort.

– What kids are you talking about?

– The Murtaghs, the Kellys, the O'Neills.

– Is that so now? And tell me how many kids have they got?

There was no point proceeding further with the selection of families that contained only one or two offspring. Arguing only produced the usual litany of complaints from their mother.

– I've never met such an ungrateful crowd. I work my fingers to the bone and all I get is whining when you're asked to do a hand's turn. Oh yes, and when I'm worn out and gone there'll be a few crocodile tears. Would you ever get out of my sight. I'll do it myself.

That was the worst part because it made them feel guilt, a pervasive emotion. They would shamefacedly pick up the dishcloth and continue. But this still left the internecine battle over precisely whose turn it was.

– I did it last night.

– No, you didn't.

– Yes I did. We had beans and (*sotto voce*) you farted all night.

– 'Beans, beans, good for the heart,
   The more you eat, the more you fart.'

– Mammy, Joe is saying curses.

– That's not a curse, you eejit.

– It's just as bad. Anyway, I did it last night.

– You're a little liar. You were out playing the shore.

– She did so. And I dried up after her.

– You're two liars then.

– Stop. Stop. Stop this eternal squabbling. Mother of God, what kind of children have I reared!

– She started it.

– I did not. He called me a liar.

– Stop it. My head is splitting. Both of you do it and that's final.

So it went. Whatever else they might breed, families certainly bred irritation and argumentation. Ironically, the Toners were described by Oul' Hartnett as the nicest family in the Hollow. What could the others be like? But then Larry, his eldest son, went off to Texas to be a cowboy, so anything must have been better than his own family. And hadn't Oul' Hartnett got up at five o'clock one summer's morning to free one of Dominic's regular acquisitions, a yowling pup, from the shed? Said he couldn't sleep with the noise of it. But he had to work early mornings anyway. So it had to be bad-mindedness. Dominic never forgave him and thought maybe he should head off to Texas too.

Still, the washing up had to be done. The argument continued while they worked.

– That's not clean.

– It is so.

– Are you blind? Look at that grease. I'm not drying that.

– Here. Gimme it. I was just seeing if you'd notice.

– You're an awful chancer.

– Smellyboots.

Sniff.

– Who let the banger?

– Not me.

– You're a liar.

– Who are you calling a liar? Mammy, Joe is after blowing and he's blaming it on me.

– 'A fart is a funny thing,
   It floats like the breeze,
   It lifts up the bedclothes,
   And suffocates the fleas.'

– Hmmph. You think you're funny.

If Bern, the eldest, was involved it usually meant hysterics among the younger ones. His method of driving one of his siblings frantic was simply to mutter certain names that he remembered from his reading: Zebediah Fradden, Ebenezer

Scrooge, Philpotts Bottle, as if they were in themelves epithets. There was no logic to it. Nobody could ever remember why these names so incensed them. Perhaps they were so obscure; perhaps they lent themselves to a particular tone of voice; perhaps he was simply displaying his intellectual superiority. His nickname, after all, was Know-It-All and such was his verbosity his grandmother used to say despairingly, 'The NOISE of him', while Granda Hope said he must have been vaccinated with a gramophone needle.

– Oh, too much brains, Mr Toner would say. I never met such a prevaricator and procrastinator. He'll drive me to an early grave. I always said it: a little education is a dangerous thing.

He tended to forget that he was the one who constantly extolled education as the only solution. When there was a strike of national teachers he set lessons for the children and examined them when he came home from work. It was completely unjust. All the other kids were enjoying themselves building mud huts down on the river bank. He dismissed their protests:

– Genius does what it must, intelligence does what it can! And God knows genius is thin on the ground in this place.

He tried vainly to counter what he called the gutter language of the neighbourhood by picking on words they misused and enunciating them laboriously. Worse, he forced them to learn rubbish off by heart on the pretext of speaking proper English. Some of them could repeat like clockwork, on demand: 'The circumlocutory and pleonastic cycle of oratorical sonorosity circumscribing an atom of ideality and lost in a verbal profundity.'

– What's that when it's at home? asked Joe sourly.

Mr Toner gave his wispy smile and looked pointedly at Bern.

– It means people who have verbal diarrhoea often miss the point.

– What's the point? muttered Joe. Joe always muttered.

– Don't mutter.

Bern may not have consciously absorbed these lectures in intellectual terrorism but he certainly mastered the technique.

Although he had been warned many times not to tease, he would wait until his mother left the tiny scullery or had her back turned, then quickly whisper Zebediahfraddenphilpottsbottle and dry a dish with an air of industry before the wail of anguish soared over to his mother's ears.

– Stop it you!

– I will not stab a Jew, Bern would cleverly respond.

The only time there was peace at the sink was when the eldest girl, Laura, was involved. She was calm and quiet, got on with the job and regularly took over the household when their mother was laid up. The youngest boys were at ease with her. Dominic swore he'd marry her when he grew up until his mother shocked him by asking was it because she had good legs. He thought the remark so crude that he never mentioned the subject again.

The next most gruesome job was weeding the back garden. While they could hear the other kids shouting from the river which was just over the back wall or see them going up the road on Saturday afternoons on their way to the pictures, the Toner kids had to squat in dusty rows of lettuces, cabbages and onions and halfheartedly pull at the weeds. The only diversion was spying on each other to report malingering or worse.

– Ma, he ate an onion.

– Shurrup, you.

– I will not. Ma, he ate a big onion.

Their mother would glance wearily through the scullery window.

– You were warned not to eat them onions; there's few enough of them. Do you want me to get the stair-rod? Wait till I tell your father.

– I didn't eat an onion.

– You did so, you dirty liar. I seen you. You'll have to tell it in confession.

– (Whispered smugly) It wasn't an onion. It was a scallion.

– Ma, he's after eating a scallion.

– Go way, you little squealer, I'll break your neck.

– You and what army? You couldn't catch a fly.

There ensued a chase through the small patch which caused

enough damage to outweigh any good done through weeding. Of course such lawlessness would never be tried if their father was at home. His presence and the threat of summary physical punishment maintained law and order. Even in his absence, the threat of reporting to him had a powerful braking effect. He was usually tired and irritable when he arrived home and the litany of offenses made him worse.

They purchased coal every autumn, their mother reckoning precisely how much they would need to supplement the cinders from the nearby Corporation plot to keep the livingroom fire glowing all day, every day and the one in the sittingroom occasionally cheerful for visitors.

When the coal was delivered she would stand behind the front curtains, motionless except for her lips which moved as if in prayer. She was scrupulously counting every bag as it was shouldered round the back. She maintained the coalman had become rich through shortchanging people who didn't count their bags. The children studied the unfortunate man to see what riches could do to a person. They saw a grimy cloth cap, a tattered sack tied around his shoulders and a face from which the ingrained coaldust could never completely be removed. They realised money wasn't everything. But the man had a fine line in obscenity when kids hung on to the back of the cart. Those for whom there wasn't room at the back would fall away yelling 'Scut the whip, scut the whip' to spoil it for the successful ones. Then a blue torrent poured from the coalman's lips as he heaved viciously on the reins, jumped down and chased the pests away.

When the coal was used up in summer it left the shed empty enough to be used as a hiding place and, on one immortal occasion, as the scene of Dominic's first kiss with Maria Magrath, a beauty with Shirley Temple ringlets. Afterwards he was so exhilarated that he ran the length of the river bank exulting in his youth and strength. He was eight at the time. He hardly felt his mother's heavy hand when she belted him for getting coaldust all over his short pants.

Except for one black winter when they had to go out gathering sticks in a blizzard, or cutting down trees and manhandling them across the Dodder, the family was never short of fuel. They had two inexpensive sources. The first was turf. During the war some people were able to rent a bog in the Dublin mountains. On Sunday mornings the men from the Hollow, accompanied by whichever children would not be a nuisance and might be a help, climbed onto a lorry which drove them up to the Featherbed mountain. There they spent the day learning the culchie art of turf-cutting.

When it was cut and spread and footed and dried and put in small ricks and then loaded on the lorries, it was bonanza time for the children. Word spread fast when a household had its turf delivered. It was dumped on the path and swarms of children descended like an army of ants to carry it into the owner's back garden. Nobody would dream of stacking the turf in the front garden. That would be completely tasteless, something a culchie might do although even the Mayo family respected the local tradition: front gardens were for hedges, a lawn and roses.

The tradition suited the children because it created employment. The trick was to catch the owner's eye every time you passed with an armful of sods of turf so that he would remember you when he was doling out rewards of pennies and tuppences. Where the Mayo family fell down was in paying the kids with lemonade. Worse, it was homemade lemonade. The following year they had to bring the turf in unaided. It was strictly a money economy here and kids made no exceptions.

The Toners actually went through the agony of turfcutting and gathering only once and that culminated in Mr Toner plunging up to his oxters in a boghole. While he struggled in the clinging mud, fuming and freezing, Joe, *mar dhea*, innocently asked him to feel around with his feet to see was there 'ere a keg of bog butter buried there'. The turf they saved was not worth the effort. It was wet and couldn't be lit. They decided you had to be born a culchie to do the job right.

But the family's greatest fuel asset was the Corporation Plot. Across the river from the Hollow a small tract of land was divided into allotments and rented to those who had the nominal rent and the considerable energy to grow vegetables. But its value consisted less in food than fuel. Apparently it had been a dumping ground for some ancient coalburning industry and the ground was largely constituted of industrial cinders. When these were sieved from the clay and used on the fire they glowed with a magnificent heat. They were a godsend during those lean years.

It was hard work separating the cinders from the pebbles but their mother paid them a penny-halfpenny for each bucketful brought home safely on the go-kart. This magnificent contraption, though constructed by Mr Toner for the children's pleasure, became indispensable for the new industry. It boasted four pram wheels and a seat and even had reins with which to steer.

The youngest child jeopardised this lucrative activity one day when he was trusted to bring the go-kart home on his own. He met an older child who offered him a 'wing' for it. As he knew only angels had wings it seemed a good bargain. He handed over the family's entire transport system and took the penny home proudly to present to his shocked parents. Fortunately he remembered that the purchaser was one of the rough Doyles from Rathfarnham, so Mr Toner and his two older sons were able to go and repossess it.

The go-kart had its uses as an ambulance also, to carry the wounded home to their mother. The children were not normally prone to sickness but by virtue of their robust lives as well as their numbers they had a high statistical incidence of cut fingers, sprained ankles, scratched faces, black eyes, as well as more dramatic wounds.

One evening in the Plots, Bern, who had become interested in field athletics, decided they would have a javelin contest. It should really have been called a trident contest because they used their father's four-pronged garden fork which he had left behind that day and which they had been sent to retrieve. Bern easily threw it furthest but, to his disgust, could not get his best throw to remain stuck in the ground. Joe, next in age, had less distance but won because his throw remained upright. Dominic became bored because he could achieve neither distance nor adherence so he invented the game of chicken: standing in the firing line and dodging the missile at the last moment. This inhibited the javelin throwers and Joe in particular who had no patience with messers.

Joe was perfectly normal but in this family's rigid code of respectability he was considered the wild one. The family mythology claimed that he hadn't spoken a word until he was two. Then one day Mr Toner lost patience and slapped him, whereupon Joe turned and said, 'Dirty Daddy', to the wild delight of his parents. He was the one who first smoked cigarettes and was seen talking to mots outside the Classic cinema. He had little interest in school, particularly in the compulsory Irish.

His parents worried that he would turn out to be a hardchaw, a gurrier, a cornerboy or slag. He was the first to use 'Corporation hairoil', or water, to achieve a quiff in his hair and was called a mickeydazzler because of it. He was often singled out for criticism which of course had the effect of making him live up to his reputation as a hardchaw.

When he wasn't looking for Joe to give him a hiding, Mr Toner would grudgingly mutter:'Sometimes I think he's the only sane one among you.' Being a bit of a misfit in this culture himself, he may have envied the natural street wisdom and humour of Joe.

On that evening in the Plots, Joe became impatient with Dominic and began to chase him with the fork, throwing it just short of the squealing boy's heels. Dominic ran for his life. It was the worst thing to do. For Joe a moving target was much more fun than throwing into space so he pursued his small brother, brilliantly missing the flying heels by inches. Inevitably Dominic gave up at the wrong moment and stopped suddenly, pleading for mercy. But the fork was already on its way and neatly impaled his right heel to the ground.

He was too shocked to cry. Joe was too appalled to move. Bern came up and pulled the fork out.

– What did you do that for?

– He shouldn't have stopped.

– Here, pull your sock down. Let's see if it's bad. My God it's pouring.

– Listen, Dominic, it was an accident, wasn't it? Sure Jasus I wouldn't try to kill you, you know that.

Dominic looked doubtfully at both of them. It was a new situation: his two big brothers worrying about him. The rule was: except as a nuisance, as in this case, younger siblings did not exist outside the home. Normally they would have nothing to do with Dominic nor, indeed, with each other. In this jungle to refer to the concept of a united family was rubbish.

The reason was practical. Life was a series of scrapes occasioned by doing those exciting things which were expressly forbidden. Younger kids always gave the game away, perhaps innocently, but nonetheless with the deadly consequences of parental retribution. 'How many times have I told you not to climb trees in your good clothes, not to play football in them shoes, not to swim with that cold on you, not to play with those kids, etc. And don't deny it. You were seen.' (At this point murderous looks were exchanged with appropriate sibling.) 'Now you can go straight to bed and wait till your father comes home. Oh ho you'll find out, me bucko, when I say no I mean no. I've never met such a disobedient crowd in all my life, I swear to God almighty.'

This was the reason Bern, being the eldest, seemed so concerned at this miserable worm's condition.

– I'll be blamed too.

Joe was on the alert.

– Whaddya mean, too? It was your idea. You started throwing the fecking thing.

– Not at him I didn't.

– Anyway it's his own fault for moving when he shouldn't have. Listen. It was an accident, okay. Dom, do you hear? We'll think of something. She'll murder you too, you know.

Dominic was torn between the emerging ache in his foot and the prospect of his mother's wrath. He nodded dumbly. Joe put an arm around his shoulder, an unheard of action.

– Good man, Dom. There's no squealers in our family, right?

They limped him out of the Plots, placed him on the go-kart and began the slow procession homewards, Bern and Joe inventing and discarding alibis as they went. Dominic held the offending fork by his side and felt like King Neptune as the other children surrounded them with questions about the source, cause and seriousness of the red blob which was Dominic's heel. The probable degree of pain was estimated as memories were jogged to find precedents and comparisons for such a wound. Dominic was reasonably mollified by their curiosity and said, 'Nah, it didn't hurt that much', although he couldn't resist closing his eyes experimentally and gritting his teeth like Hopalong Cassidy when the arrow was being pulled out of his arm. It was nice being a hero for a change.

The only worry he had was whether Mrs Toner would put a hot poultice on his foot. That was the most terrible cure of all, used as a last resort on boils.

Whenever an accident happened there was always some smart aleck who would run ahead to seize some of the glory by being the first to tell the news. So their mother was waiting at the door, arms folded, eyes moving heavenward in time to her tsk, tsk, tsks.

– What is it this time? Jesus, Mary and Joseph, you can't be let out on a simple message but one of you comes back in flitters. Now what is it? Let me see that. Sure it's only a scratch. Where's all the blood coming from? Merciful God, what happened to you? Your good sock is ruined. Oh, God in heaven, look at that. There's a hole through his foot. What are you two doing, standing gawking there? Get the basin and water and the dettol, no, the iodine.

As they had hoped, she was too busy with the injury – washing it carefully, telling the boy to stop jumping before she even touched it with iodine, wrapping a bandage torn from an old sheet round heel and instep – to conduct an immediate inquiry. Thus Bern and Joe were able to get in their story of seeing a massive rat in the Plots and bravely trying to kill it until their idiot brother ran straight into the path of the fork.

Dominic had been so carefully rehearsed on the way home that by now he could almost see the rat. He said nothing and looked brave. Mrs Toner was suspicious but what could she do? Bern and Joe relaxed as she rose from her knees. She shook her head resignedly.

– I do not know. I really do not know.

Dominic's only regret was that they were already on holidays so he couldn't get off school. Still, he didn't have to pick cinders, wash the dishes or weed the garden for a while. It wasn't altogether a wasted wound.

· SIX ·

MRS TONER HAD NO TIME FOR FINICKY EATERS, particularly on Fridays. 'You'll follow the crows for that good food,' she would say.

– I hate fish.

– Well you're not getting anything else. Do you not know that fish give you brains!

Yes, and so did cold tea. And carrots were good for their eyes. And porridge built muscles. And the skin of the potato was the best part; that's where all the vitamins from the sun were stored. All of the devious ways to get them to eat. But don't eat the skin of an orange because it'll give you yellow jaundice. And sugar gives you worms and if you eat enough lard or dripping you'll get sick and won't have to go to school – and does your mother keep dripping? Well, get her a plumber.

– Ah, Mammy, can I have a bit of bread then?

– Not until you've eaten every scrap of that fish.

– But it's horrible looking.

– I didn't say it was an oil painting and I didn't ask you to look at it. Just eat it.

One day Bern got an imitation rubber spider and left it in his mother's cup of tea when they departed back to school after their dinner. She said it nearly gave her a heart attack and told Mr Toner who gave Bern a clatter.

– You better develop some respect for your mother, young fellow-me-lad.

They developed expressions of revolt.

'Don't eat Kennedys' bread
It sticks to your belly like lead.
You fart like thunder

Your mother doesn't wonder
Don't eat Kennedys' bread.'
– Do you not know there are children starving in the world
that would give their left eye for such a tasty dinner?
– Why don't you give the fish to them, then?
– None of your impudence now. You're not getting another
scrap until you eat that.
There would follow some fiddling, foostering, playing with
knife, fork, plate, obnoxious contents.
– Mammy, can I have a bit of bread to mop it up?
– I said it before and I'll say it again. You're not filling
yourself up with bread. It'll ruin your dinner.
'Bolands' bread will kill a man dead
Especially a man with a baldy head.'
Allowing for the fact that normal children are constantly
hungry anyway they didn't do too badly in those straitened
times.
– You're better off than most, said Mr Toner. A good diet is
the key to perfect health. Good wholesome food and plenty of
exercise, you can't beat it. Look at dogs. They only have one
meal a day. Have you ever seen a sick dog?
– Yes, and you can tell they're sick 'cause they've a dry nose.
– Ah, but that's only because some fool has given them
sweets or something. If we could live like dogs we'd be much
healthier.
– They get the mange and die at twelve, muttered Joe.
– That's seventy in human terms, corrected Mr Toner. And
even then they can still chase cats. Can you see your grandfather chasing cats?
– He wouldn't be that much of an eejit.
– That's not the point. Your Mammy and I are perfectly
satisfied that you get plenty to eat. Anything else is sheer greed.
Whatever their perfect diet was, it was not enough and had
to be supplemented with sweets, gurcakes, stolen fruit and
anything else they could forage. They still tended to get con-
stipated and worse, they got worms.
– Mammy, I want to do me nammy.
– You're for an enema tonight.
– Ah no, Mammy.

– Oh yes, Mammy. I saw you scratching. Besides, you're crawling with worms.

Mrs Toner had eyes like a secretary bird, could spot the tiny white worms wriggling frantically in their stools, the result of too much sugar filched surreptitiously with wet fingers from the bowl. The enema was to flush the worms out and also to loosen their bowels when a poor diet made them constipated.

It was a grotesque procedure which must eliminate forever the possibility of human pretension. What sublimated pleasure did she derive? She laid them in turn on their stomachs on the ironing board, pushed a rubber tube with a bulbous end up their backsides and squirted a salt and water solution into them. It worked instantly and they queued up for the potty. Their reward for enduring the indignity was a sweet. Little did they know at the time that it too contained a laxative.

It was just another of the million and one responsibilities that lay on the thin shoulders of Mrs Toner. Her husband was responsible for exterior jobs, like fixing bikes, digging the garden, painting the exterior doors and windows. She was responsible for the interior, which included pasting up new wallpaper as well as keeping the house shipshape.

Every week she piled all the chairs on the table and began the task of polishing the linoleum in the livingroom, hall and kitchenette. The smell was lovely but it was a bit disturbing to see her straining her slight body, pausing often to straighten her back, mop her brow, push a wisp of hair back and, deep breath, sigh, start again. She had no worksongs. The best part was when she tied rags to their stockinged feet and let them slide up and down to polish the floor. There was no pay for it but they didn't mind. It reminded them of winter when they poured water on the road outside and had to wait only a short time before it froze and they had hours of enjoyment on the slide until the inevitable crank or saboteur from up the road sprinkled salt and ruined it.

Come to think of it, except for Easter and Christmas and the penny a week on Saturdays there was no pay for anything. 'Do you think I'm made of money! It doesn't grow on trees, you know. Isn't it enough that you have a good home, three meals a day and your faith?'

Think of the pagan children starving in Africa who hadn't even the consolation of religion although our missionaries were working on it. The children thought that if they kept all the pennies they had been forced to squander on black babies they wouldn't be poor themselves. But it wouldn't do to voice such a thought, especially not to the nuns who collected the pennies. The Sunday evening radio appeal was costly too. Once there was a particularly harrowing one about a leper colony run by Fr Damian on Molokai in the Pacific.

– What's a 'lepper'?
– It's unfortunate people with a terrible disease that makes their limbs fall off.
– How can they 'lep' if they're like that?
– They don't lep. They walk around slowly.
– Why are they called 'leppers', then?
– Would you not be asking idiotic questions.

Mr Toner put a half-crown on the table and invited them to contribute some of their pocket money to the cause. Pocket money, how are ye! Slowly and grudgingly the pennies and thruppenny pieces were produced. It was to teach them the necessity of charity, but never did knowledge enter so painfully. When they got a note back from the recipients praising their wonderful kindness they didn't feel too bad but they made themselves scarce when future radio appeals were broadcast lest their father have another attack of charity on their behalf.

The only times they could be sure of having money were Christmas and Easter when fortunes were made cleaning windows – properly, mind you; the brasses on the windows had to be made to gleam like gold; then the firegrate had to be freshly blacked, the kitchen sink to be purged with bleach, all shelves to be lined with fresh newspaper. Each job had its own rate. The silver in the glasscase was at a premium and was reserved for the older kids. It was the only time the precious tea set, a wedding present from Granny and Granda Hope, saw the light of day.

Every picture in the house was taken down and dusted and the glass washed. If anybody was caught lingering over the one in the sittingroom above the piano they were pitilessly mocked. It was a print entitled 'Daybreak'; the painter was Maxfield Parrish and it featured what they remembered as two naked women in a Grecian setting. One woman was bending over the other, hands on her knees, thighs pressed together so there wasn't really much to see. She was waking the other who lay stretched out on the concrete or marble or whatever it was. The main curiosity was how they didn't catch their death of cold, that there was a place in the world where people could sleep naked out in the open. But it was also an opportunity to see nude women. They had seen one of their Aunt Emily's tits once when she was feeding her baby. It was only a glimpse before they were ushered from the room. It was huge. Aunt Emily was embarrassed. So were they.

When Maisie McGee offered to swap a glimpse of her bum for a look at Damo Scully's weewee man, it caused a sensation. The story spread like wildfire but she wouldn't repeat the offer to the many other potential takers. Who cares, they said. She's only a big lump anyway.

In that sense the picture was educational. It was also daring and would not have been tolerated had it not been a wedding present from their other granny.

When Mrs Toner referred with unmistakeable coolness to 'that picture' they knew exactly what she was thinking. A picture, I ask you! Just what a newly-married couple living on £2 a week needed as a wedding present.

The difference between the picture and the equally impractical tea service was underlined by attitudes towards the reciprocal grandparents.

– I wouldn't mind but he still goes over to his mother's house on a Friday night and opens his paypacket there. I've never seen it. It's not as if she needed the money. She's living with her daughter and has the pension. You'd think his first

59

responsibility would be to his own family. Oh no. She never let go of him. He kept her from the time he was sixteen.

She said this just once and probably regretted it but children clutch at all straws to understand their world. It became a stroke in the slow, gradual etching that formed their world picture.

It was hard to match their mother's opinion with their visits to Granny Toner. She was small and white-haired with a broad upper lip like their father – he called it the Milesian lip – plus black eyebrows and spectacles just like him. She also had an intriguing trace of a moustache.

She would sit at her piano, drape her pinafore over the keys and to their astonishment play 'Yankee Doodle Dandy' with the right hand and 'The Camptown Races' with the other. At the same time. With her eyes closed. She also had an infectious chuckle.

They all had to sing on these New Year's Day visits. Laura played 'The Robin's Return'. Joe told a joke. None of them got the point of it but their relatives laughed heartily and said he was a card. Their uncle was a lovely man who chain-smoked and had a nice grin and plenty of riddles.

– What's under the water and over the water but never in the water?

– I give up.

– An egg in a duck's belly.

– What's the difference between a duck?

– What!

– You heard.

– I give up.

– 'Cause one of its legs is both the same.

– What! That's not a proper answer.

– Okay. Here's one: a flea and a fly in a flue were trapped so what could they do?

– (Excitedly) Give up. What's a flue?

– Don't mind that. Do you give up?

– Yes.

– Said the flea let us fly, said the fly let us flee, so they flew through a flaw in the flue.

– Another.

– Okay, but don't tell your father this one. Do you promise?

– (Chorus) Yeah!

– What's the difference between a seagull and a baby?

Aunt Emily frowned warningly. He shrugged. They clamoured.

– What? Tell us.

– I'll tell you the first part: One flits along the shore and...

– Go on. Finish it.

– Finish it yourselves.

Bern, the brains of the family, thought hard, then whispered to Joe, who said convulsed:

– The other shits along the floor!

Aunt Emily put an end to it.

– All right. Another song now.

Aunt Emily was Mr Toner's sister and she was a champion step-dancer who had millions of medals to prove it, not that she could dance with the weight of them on, but they saw the photos. They also studied the photo of their dead grandfather in his tradesman's apron with a bowler hat and big moustache which must have been where Granny Toner got hers but they saw no sign that he was a drunkard, which was a disappointment.

They were pumped full of Christmas cake and pudding and lemonade and when they were leaving with pockets full of sixpences and sweets they were showered with the blessings of every saint in heaven, God's Holy Mother, gallons of holy water and the final 'May He keep you all safe in the hollow of His Hand'.

What could their mother be talking about? These relatives were smashing. It took a long time for the tension between the in-laws to seep into their consciousness and then it was like an invisible mist of which they could never be fully aware. Coincidentally, three of the Toner kids were dark like their mother and the other three had the fair hair and freckled look of their father's family. This tended to separate them into factions when crises emerged and tensions erupted.

There was no television to provide surrogate drama, to supply images of alternative realities, however banal, to the inescapable opinions, judgements and presence of parents and in-laws. Theirs was the children's only reality. Their tensions too. The experience of the cinema was too infrequent to mediate its illusions. It only served as an occasional escape from reality.

It was years before they met Mrs Toner's sister who had reared a family in England. 'More pigmen,' Mr Toner would say out of his wife's hearing.

The English branch of the tribe was the result of Aunt Colleen, Granda Hope's other daughter, eloping with a British Tommy after the Irish War of Independence.

– They should have shaved her head, said Mr Toner out of the corner of his mouth.

Judgemental as ever. Where did it come from, this hard dismissiveness? It did not match the treacle of his songs. Was it simply an automatic defence, evolved in a time and place where to show one's gentler feelings was to be open to ridicule? They must be camouflaged, to emerge in gruffness or sublimated into saccharine song. And what effect must this have had on the soft putty of their childhood?

The soldier's name was also Tommy, and love was inevitable when Colleen found out his family kept pigs in Berkshire. From this liaison came the most exciting cousin any children could hope for: a sailor in the British Navy. His job during the war was to swim away from the mother ship, the *HMS Indefatigable* and travel miles to fix mines to enemy ships. He was called a frogman and was infinitely superior to Rockfist Rogan in the comics.

He was a god of nineteen when he arrived on leave and they were allowed to stay up late one summer's night when he said he wanted a swim. They all trooped up with their father to the bridge and couldn't believe it when the cousin plunged into the black, eel-inhabited waters. He didn't seem to realise that this was the time the otters came out too, and they could take the leg off you.

He emerged safely at the bank and looked up at the bridge.

– Is there enough water to go off the top? he asked in his funny accent.

He couldn't be serious.

But he was. They followed this dripping god of war, their very own Biggles, Dan Dare and Johnny Weissmuller all rolled into one. They held their breath as he balanced on the top parapet and then dived. The tremendous splash was followed by total silence. They couldn't see through the twilight. Had he surfaced? Maybe he'd gone too deep and his head was stuck in the mud? What a miserable way to go. They rushed down to the bank of the river and peered anxiously around. No sign. They shook their heads at the black, oily depths. It looked very different in the bright early morning sunshine. Then a white hand emerged slowly like the Creature from the Black Lagoon and gave them a fright. They shouted as his head bobbed up, grinning. He must have been hours underneath. Of course – hadn't he been trained to swim for miles underwater, carrying bombs, too.

This cousin had pockets full of money and was dying to give it all away. Funny how when they played 'sevens' at night with him he seemed to win it all back. But they didn't really mind. Easy come, easy go.

The rest of the English branch of the family followed in dribs and drabs. They learned with amazement that their aunt Colleen, a mother of four, also worked in a factory. England was a very queer place.

– I always said it. A pagan country. No respect for the family or the sacred role of motherhood. What kind of rearing is that for kids? A woman's place is in the home.

Their relatives had accents like you'd hear on comedy programmes on the BBC. They took enormous pleasure in eating rashers and black pudding and plastering their bread with butter. Mrs Toner said they'd been half-starved during the war, God love them, and they were entitled to make up for it. They brought their other children, Philip and Joan with them. These two weren't nearly as exciting as their sailor brother, nor as generous, but it was still bonanza time. Just for showing them the way to Granny's house in Churchtown they got a shilling. For doing nothing at all they got pennies. Fortunes were made in that week.

To mark the visit the Toners had a party and invited all the tribe, not that there were that many. All came except Granny Toner who pleaded another attack of asthma. Their mother looked relieved when she heard this and moved the dinner table on its side out into the hall to make room for dancing.

There was no limit to the lemonade and cakes, and their father sang 'The Floral Dance' as good as Peter Dawson. Even Granda Hope sang for the first time in their hearing:

'As I was awalking down No-orth Ki-ing Street
A bould recruiting sergeant I chanced for to meet.
He enlisted me,
Aye and he traced me, aye and he forced me to roam,
To the Queen's royal barracks, boys,
He fo-erced me to roam.'

A few of the adults knew the chorus:

'Cold irons, cold irons, cold irons on me,
I was handcuffed, strongly guarded boys,
Cold irons on me.'

Cousin Philip danced with Laura all night and she ignored her siblings' nudges and winks. She looked very poised. Their aunt, the champion step-dancer, gave the performance of her life, hands tight to her side, feet flashing in and out, knees jerking up in the air in the middle of a twirl. They all sang da-da, da-da, da-da, diddle-diddle da-da and clapped their hands to give her a rhythm. And of course they speeded it up so she ended at fifty miles an hour in a state of collapse. Granda Hope caught her in his arms, swung her around and cried, 'I never reared a jibber.' That was a great compliment for a pony. Even Mr Toner couldn't conceal his pleasure that his sister had shown the Toner side of the family to be the more talented.

It was the best night any of them could remember and they were let stay up right to the very end when cousin Joan was eventually coaxed – they'd been working on it all night – to sing. She began in a reedy voice.

'With someone like you, a pal so good and true,
I'd like to leave it all behind and go and find
A place that's known to God alone,
Just a spot to call our own
We'd find perfect peace where joys would never cease ...'

Her voice wobbled and distracted them from contemplation of the paradise. Aunt Emily gushed as was her wont: 'Go on, darling. Oh hasn't she a lovely voice?'

'And there beneath the kind starlight,
We'd build a sweet little nest ...'

This time the wobble was serious. Auntie Colleen whispered something to Mrs Toner who nodded, smiling, satisfied, just as she'd guessed, like they'd all guessed, that Joan had a boyfriend in England and was head over heels in love with him and missed him. It was just like the pictures. Ah, romance. They all made encouraging noises, she got out the bit about 'a little nest somewhere in the West' and they all drowned her with the last line:

'AND LET THE REST OF THE WORLD GO BY.'

Thunderous applause followed.

Then they all went home and the children went to bed to relive in whispers every second of the magic evening.

Not long after their relatives returned to England, Laura began to receive letters from Philip. They caused excitement because they were real letters and tension because they were love letters. One evening after tea all the kids except Laura were evicted from the diningroom and the door was shut tight. They took turns at the hole in the floor above but couldn't make sense of the conversation. Eventually Laura rushed out, ran up the stairs and slammed her bedroom door. They heard noises that sounded like sobbing which was unheard of for her.

They knew of course that she must be madly in love with Philip but it was out of the question because first cousins, any cousins, can't marry. It was against religion apart from the fact that it produces lunatic children and worse, hairy, two-headed things that have to be put in the dustbin before anybody could see them. It had something to do with priests as well. Some things in life were beyond debate and this was one of them. Besides, Laura was only about sixteen and had millions of fellows after her. She'd never end up an old maid in Portland Row. Dominic was once cycling down the Rathgar Road with her and saw her smiling acknowledgment of the wolf whistles from men digging a trench. He expressed disapproval but she just smiled at him and said the poor hardworking men were entitled to a bit of diversion.

Later on she met another young man on a train who also wrote long letters to her. But he was an even more hopeless case – a Protestant. Laura was finally coached in a long and sincere letter which said that as a Catholic it would be wrong to continue to encourage his hopes because of her unshakeable conviction in her religion which was the One True Faith; of course she respected the sincerity with which he adhered to his own beliefs no matter how mistaken and she would pray for the grace of God to enlighten him. She thanked him for his flattering attentions and hoped and prayed that some day he would obtain the Gift of Faith when they might resume the correspondence. Until then it would be unwise to do so.

On the back of the envelope Laura inscribed, as was the custom, the initials S.A.G. which stood for 'St Anthony guide'. Even the postal service occasionally needed a little spiritual help.

The young man never replied. He probably realised that however he might get around Laura's unshakeable faith, he did not stand a snowball's chance in hell against the flowery prose of Mr Toner.

SEVEN

ONCE EVERY TWELVE MONTHS THEY HAD A VISIT from Mr Toner's distant cousin the priest.

He was one of the few missionaries in Africa who hadn't been eaten by cannibals, he said. He was their personal link with the black babies and he had a loud laugh. They had mixed feelings about him because he refused to show them his John Thomas. This was his weapon for controlling the unruly kids in his classroom in Nigeria and he carried it in a shoulder holster under his armpit, but he wouldn't take it out, said it would frighten them too much. They were used to straps and canes and the nuns' belts in school, so this must be studded with nails and razor blades or hooks to pull the veins out of your wrists. Pity the poor black babies. This man never brought sweets, just medals blessed by the pope and little badges like the ones in their father's locker, the ones in the shape of a dove which represented the Holy Ghost. The medals were useless unless you could persuade the unsuspecting that they were made of silver and get a coloured marble in return.

When they asked Father Eddie where he worked he called for the *Book of Knowledge*, volume A-D for Africa, pointed a finger at a blank space on the Dark Continent and said: 'There, that's where I am.'

They looked and saw lions and elephants and dinosaurs, savages, a boiling sun and they wondered how this man could survive in his black suit. They supposed that was the price he paid for living in a country where it was so hot you could swim all the year round if you minded out for the crocodiles and particularly the piranha fish which would strip the flesh off you in thirty seconds so that all that was left were your white bones drifting to the bottom with nothing to hold them together.

– Do black babies have black bones too? they asked.

– Not at all, he said. The only difference between them and us is the colour of their skin.

He was interesting on such subjects. They looked with renewed respect at this visitor. That's why they didn't mind him not bringing sweets.

Besides, all visitors were a welcome diversion from the ordinary. They represented a truce, a suspension of normal hostilities in the home. The parents displayed the children proudly as if they had not been threatening to skin them alive five minutes before. Many a knock on the door had brought a reprieve. And of course, the morning after visitors, you could dash down to the sittingroom and you might find a coin fallen down by the side cushions of the Chesterfield armchair. So, on the whole, visitors were welcome.

Even the siblings were polite to each other – more like ignoring each other – for the duration of the visit although there was the normal, silent but vicious elbowing for the best place near the visitor if he or she had sweets. So, just like Oul' Hartnett, visitors got the impression of the ideal family, lots of happy kids, hardworking simple parents, a clean home.

They knew better. They knew what happy homes were. They read about them in books: homes where the maximum number of kids was two, a boy and a girl who never cursed, always wore clean clothes, had a bike each, said 'Mummy' instead of Mammy, were called Jane and Jonathan, had nannies and gardeners and said 'actually' and 'I promise you' and nothing stronger than 'you rotter'. Better still, Jane and Jonathan's parents were the essence of sweet reasonableness and never lost their rag.

No wonder the children – certainly one or two of them – were sure they were foundlings or had been mixed up at birth. They could speculate on rich parents, maybe even princes, and homes with a room of their own and no brats of brothers or sisters stealing their comics or squealing on them. It was a nice daydream, a way of handling the subterranean tensions that rumbled through every day. Suppose a visitor came one day and said: 'You're really mine. I'm taking you away.' Somebody nice, in a car maybe. A woman in furs, but not a snob of course. A soft-spoken lady with rings. I mean, they'd say 'Thanks, Mammy' to their surrogate mother for minding them for so long. That would be only fair. But they'd be glad to get away, into the back of the car with a pile of all the back editions of the *Beano* and not look back at the face of Mrs Toner.

– Have you nothing better to be doing than lounging around with your nose stuck in them comics? Well you can stop daydreaming this minute and give a hand with the washing up. And if I find them comics lying around again I'll throw them in the fire.

See what I mean?

There were other visitors. The Brennock girls came about once a year: three strapping young ones up from the country, obscure cousins or friends of cousins of their father. It was clear they came from Mr Toner's side because his wife was unflattering.

– More culchies up looking for husbands. Did you see the make-up? Real glamour-pusses.

Make-up was frowned on, of course. It marked a girl as fast. They once saw their father violently rubbing lipstick off Laura's face. But she didn't cry.

He didn't do it to these girls. He was all over them, especially Marian who could play anything by ear on the piano and accompanied him when he sang. The girls also sang duets: 'Alice Where Art Thou' and 'Panis Angelicus'. Funny to think they were culchies. They didn't wear brown boots. In fact their clothes were the height of fashion and they were all good lookers. Bern tried to get something going with the eldest but Mrs Toner's attitude soon cooled whatever it was. Dominic looked longingly at the next eldest because she was pink and soft and he wanted to climb into her lap. As she was about ten years older than him nothing came of that either.

As far as they could gather, Mrs Toner's coolness towards visitors was based on both economics and fatigue. Having spent the day cooking and cleaning for eight, she was worn out and visitors were the last straw. If a knock came on the door after tea, she would look to heaven and say, tsk, tsk, who in God's name is it now? Apart from the extra labour of preparing tea and biscuits and forced smiles, there was the economic factor: I'm not the Queen of England. I can't afford to feed every stray that comes to the door, not on what I get.

The truth was that visitors, few as they were, were usually Mr Toner's friends and relatives. Why should she be nice to them when even her principal visitor, Granda Hope, was treated with such distant politeness?

Thus even Mr Ryder, the little man with the big voice who cycled over from Dolphin's Barn occasionally to sing with their father, was treated with equally cold politeness. That such volume could come from such a small frame astonished them. 'Good goods in small parcels,' said Mr Toner.

The two friends would shut themselves up in the sitting-room with the piano although neither could play more than the first note to give them their key. Their repertoire was predictable, starting off with rousing military airs like 'The Trumpeter' or 'The Company Sergeant Major' and the like where the third verse was always in a sad, minor key – that was when the soldiers were dying – but ending on a great burst like 'The Last Chord' when they'd all rise again and get together for a party.

After that there were the more intimate songs like 'Friend O' Mine' or 'Pal of My Cradle Days', 'The Heart Bowed Down', 'Even Bravest Heart' and 'Oh Promise Me' when you could feel the emotion seeping out under the door. Having warmed up they would launch into the duets, 'The Pearl Fishers', 'The Moon Hath Raised', the one from *La Bohème* and so on. They would end, like professional recitalists, with a couple of sensitive Irish ballads arranged by Hardebeck and Hughes, things like 'The Road to Ballyshee' or 'She Moved through the Fair' or 'The Ould Plaid Shawl'.

'But peace of mind I'll never find until my own I call,
That little Irish colleen in her ould plaid shawl.'

Mr Ryder told the children that he and their father once

acted in a pantomime where Mr Toner had to roll down the aisle on a barrel, then leap onto the stage shouting 'Christopher Columbus' for some reason neither could remember. It was a new light on their father. If only they'd seen him. If only, just once more, he went into a pantomime. Mr Toner nodded resignedly. Marriage puts an end to that gallivanting.

The pair of them nodded ruefully and the children wondered if adults ever continued doing what they enjoyed. They always seemed to be moaning about the good old days and what might have been and so forth.

To emphasise the point Mr Toner then sang 'When Your Days of Philandering Are Over', which he seemed to have forgotten was by the despised composer, Mozart, whose instrumental works he described as inspired doodling. Come to think of it, he also sang an aria from *Il Seraglio*, also by Mozart:

'When a maiden you have chosen, who is
fairer than a flower,
Let your kisses rain upon her, be a man
that she can honour,
Or her love won't last an hour.'

Adults are very inconsistent.

Apart from these few, there weren't many visitors. The Toners didn't have millions of relations like everybody else.

Dominic could not remember anything of the uncle after whom he was named and who was reputed to be a good looker who got a bang of a football on the head at a match and died of meningitis. And he was only a spectator, which proved that you knew not the day nor the hour and that the picture in their Granny's of Jesus with a crown of thorns and a lantern knocking on some unfortunate's door in the middle of the night was no joke. I'm coming to get you, Jesus was saying, and I'm not taking no for an answer.

Mr Toner tried to explain the oddity of being killed by a football.

– It's like an eggshell, the human skull, you could crush it like that. He slammed his palms together, ruining his *Irish Press* in the demonstration, but the noise it made was effective.

71

That's why boxing is a barbaric sport and should be banned. So don't be getting into scraps.

Pity he didn't think about that when he was clouting them.

Even though Dominic knew in his heart and soul that it was Jesus who killed everybody including his uncle, he still had nightmares of huge spheres, not footballs, more like planets, rumbling down on top of him in a vast open space with no shelter and him running like hell with nowhere to hide from the searchlights and the spheres crunching along behind him, steadily catching up, ready to squash him flat like the flour under his mother's rolling pin except that blood would squirt out from every corner of him like a fly under a rolled newspaper. He had that nightmare for years.

Then there was Granda Hope's other son, Tom. According to their mother he had married beneath him. He had a good job in a shop in Grafton Street, the place Mrs Toner served her time as a milliner before she gave up her independence and devoted herself to six ungrateful kids and what thanks did she get, I ask you? Feck all, that's what. Still, God's holy will be done, sigh. Why did Uncle Tom have to go and marry a servant girl, a skivvy, if you like? In this culture all kettles called all pots black. He didn't have to marry her, like, you know, nudge, it wasn't one of them marriages; they had no children.

They did not often meet Uncle Tom outside the home and he rarely visited them. What they knew was that he was a great golfer and won his Christmas dinner every year. Not that they ever saw any of this largesse, as their mother offhandedly mentioned. She always used the careful tone when speaking of him which they easily interpreted as disapproval of his high living and the implication that he didn't look after his aged parents as well as she did. Oh yes. He has a great life. And why wouldn't he, with no kids to bother him?

That echoed disturbingly. You wouldn't want to be too thin-skinned. At least Uncle Tom was direct in his comments, like his laughing remark after inspecting Dominic: 'He might be all right but he has the head of a bloody rogue.'

Dominic worried about that for a long time too, studied his

shadow on the ground to see the shape of his head. In moonlight his head looked smaller, more normal. But then, there always seemed to be something to worry about. He had a kind of mental list of the ordeals he had to survive and as they happened he crossed them off and braced himself for the next. What a life.

Uncle Tom also drank whiskey. You could tell from the red veins on his cheekbones. His wife drank sherry and developed a great cackle after two, but she was all right, not bad.

Uncle Tom had one advantage. He had been a stretcher-bearer in the First World War and told them great stories about waiting for a lull in the firing to slip out into no-man's land and pick up corpses. Of course the firing always resumed before they got back to the trench so they had to duck and run a lot. They saw photos of him in uniform, a gangly youngster with a cigarette in his mouth to make him look older. He spent three Christmasses in the trenches. They knew this from the fancy cards which he sent to Granny Hope, 'My own dear mother, with love from her fond son, Tom', and the stamp of the censor on them.

Uncle Tom never brought sweets or slipped them a coin, which was strange when you thought about it. He called on them with his wife one Hallowe'en dressed in masks and frightened the life out of them. But people who did this were themselves looking for sweets or money so it was hard to understand. Maybe his money all went on drink and golf about which they knew nothing except it was played by snobs in plus fours up in Milltown. Oh yes, they also knew a few words of Frank Crommett's song:

'... Oh the dirty little pill went rolling down the hill
And rolled right into the bunker ...'

which they always mixed up with 'Granny's Old Armchair' by the same singer. They knew all the words of that:

'How they tittered, how they laughed,
How my brothers and my sisters chaffed,
When they heard the lawyer declare,
Granny's left you her old armchair.

In the song the smug siblings get a comeuppance at the end when the chair turns out to be stuffed with pound notes. Maybe that's why the song interested the children, each identifying with the lucky inheritor of the chair.

One day they came home from school to find their mother weeping and a neighbour comforting her.

– Don't be always thinking the worst. Of course it was an accident. Wasn't he a sensible man in the prime of life? What would a man in his position be wanting to do a thing like that? Hadn't he everything to live for?

Mrs Toner lifted her head mournfully and looked at her children with red eyes. She had a way of getting every bit of drama from a situation, but this time she wasn't acting.

– Your Uncle Tom is dead.

They didn't know him that well so it didn't bother them too much. But to see their mother in that state was pretty awful. On the other hand, this was interesting. What did the neighbour, Mrs O'Toole, mean when she said 'do such a thing?' Had their uncle killed somebody or robbed a bank before he died? Mrs Toner was in no fit state to be interrogated, so they had to rely on Mrs O'Toole's kids for the information. Shamey O'Toole knew it all: their Uncle Tom had been found lying on the kitchen floor with the oven door open and the gas full on. That was suspicious for a start because the Glimmer Man was always looking out for people who used gas when they weren't supposed to. There was only one startling conclusion: Uncle Tom had committed suicide.

A suicide in the family! Yippee. No other kids had such a distinction. Could it be murder? Not at all. Murders are only committed in America.

When grief had subsided and their father came home and they asked for more details they were told it was none of their business and to kneel down and pay special attention during the Rosary, Sorrowful Mysteries, for the soul of the departed. Later they overheard snatches of conversation:

– For God's sake, woman, have a bit of sense. Get a hold of yourself. Of course it was an accident. He was probably stocious when he came in. Tried to make a cup of tea. It could happen to anyone.

– A cup of tea with the oven on! And how dare you say he was stocious. He was my brother. (Sobs)

– You know what I mean. It's just that you can get dizzy coming in from the cold air after a couple. And you know these gas cookers. It's easy to switch on the wrong jet. Sure he probably slipped and banged his head.

– There wasn't a brack on him, not a mark. And the worst was he lay there all night while that one was fast asleep in bed.

– Have it your own way. If you want to think the worst ...

– That woman never looked after him properly. She didn't know how to make a home. That's why they were always out.

What was more exciting was that they knew from their religion that suicides were not let into graveyards. They had to join unbaptised infants outside in unconsecrated ground. It was tough, they knew, but if you let every Tom, Dick and Harry in what would be the point in belonging to the One True Church? If people knew they were going to be buried by priests in the normal way, no matter what they did, there'd be nothing to stop them committing suicide. It was a bit hard on babies, but then they were so young they probably wouldn't know the difference.

Anyway, babies went to Limbo which wasn't nearly as bad as hell because, although the fires were boiling, you weren't there forever. Unless the nun was lying, which was impossible. That made all the difference.

The excitement grew the following day when they heard there was going to be something called a coroner's report. If he said it was suicide then that was that: out their Uncle Tom went. But where would he be buried? In the Plots? In their Granda's back garden? The pigs might dig him up and it would be a bit scary. They couldn't bury him at sea because though he had fought in the First World War – he was the one who brought back the bullet crucifix – he was a soldier, not a sailor like their cousin. Anyway, burial at sea was a bit of a cheat because in the pictures they had seen the bodies wrapped in flags which at the last minute they were too mean to let go of and the bodies always slipped out from underneath. Too mean also to give the bodies a coffin ... at which point in their speculation Bern said not to be stupid, how could a wooden coffin sink? Well, they could always put lead in it, couldn't they? This was dismissed with the derision it deserved.

Mr and Mrs Toner came home that evening with solemn faces but they demolished their children's expectations of high drama. Death by something called 'misadventure' was the verdict.

– What's that?

– It's an accident.

It was discussed in bed at length.

– Misadwhat?

– You heard. An accident.

– Why can't they say that, then?

– Why can't they say what, then? Mind your own business. And I'll mind mine. Kiss your own sweetheart and I'll kiss mine.

– Smart aleck.

– Do you want a dig?

– You and what army? Maaammmy! He's after thumping me.

And that was that. No prolonged debates or even a decent fight about where he should be buried. It was a let-down. No possibility of him being kept on ice for a while. Hey, where would they keep him? In our house? Don't be thick. He'd be stinking in no time.

A way had been found: as an old soldier he could be buried in the military plot in Glasnevin.

– The dead centre of Dublin, said Joe.

– Ha ha, you think you're funny, don't you. You shouldn't mock the dead.

– What can they do about it?

It was disappointing.

Nevertheless a funeral is a funeral, the first for most of them and therefore something to look forward to. They deserved some compensation for having been deprived of a suicide in the family, a boast that would have earned them terrific status because, like murder, it was unheard of in this country, the grandest little, best living, happiest, holiest little country in the world. Only pagans and Swedes committed suicide, explained Mr Toner. Despite centuries of dungeon fire and sword they were sustained by their greatest strength, their Holy Faith which supplied us all with the strength to endure everything in this Vale of Tears. Unless a person went mad or lost the Faith – which amounted to the same thing – they wouldn't take their own life. Bern, of course, old rise-a-row had to mention Wolfe Tone who slit his own throat rather than submit to the hangman. Mr Toner cleared his gullet.

– A patriot, I'll give you that. One of our greatest. But as you probably know, he was not of our Faith.

Oh? An Irish patriot not a Catholic? Amazing. Nobody ever told them that before.

The funeral had its own touch of drama. Everybody was very solemn and the big green cypress trees looked like something from a film. Granny Hope's eyes were red as she and Mrs Toner supported each other on the walk down the muddy path. Granda Hope looked grim and walked by himself, not talking to anyone, not even to the children which was unusual.

Uncle Tom's widow was escorted by Mr Toner. She was near collapsing as far as they could see. The children were all dressed in their Sunday clothes. Weren't they lucky their mother didn't have to put them in pawn on a Monday and take them out on Friday like the queue of women down at Kelly's Corner. Not only did they have a day off school; they were promised lemonade and sandwiches in the house if they behaved themselves and didn't say a word and didn't squabble at the funeral. It was like Christmas.

At the graveside they watched closely as the coffin was lowered on ropes. If one of the gravediggers slipped would it land upside down? How would their uncle get out on the Last Day when he was supposed to rise, body and soul, into heaven? And why didn't gravediggers wear their good clothes like the rest of them? That spoiled things a bit.

Before the shovels started pushing the earth back in and before the priest started his prayers, their Granda unexpected-

ly pushed forward. God, was he going to jump in after his son?
He began to speak. Everybody looked startled, particularly the
priest who was supposed to be in complete control of death.

– Goodbye, Tom. I don't know and I don't care what way
you died. We all end the one way. You're gone now and
whatever else, you were a good son to me. May God have
mercy on your soul for that.

He turned away violently and pushed back into the crowd
but their sharp eyes spotted he was crying, the first time they
ever saw such a thing in a grown man. It made a couple of them
cry, too.

· EIGHT ·

THE PEOPLE FROM THE SURROUNDING OPULENCE of Rathgar and Churchtown regarded the Hollow as Indian territory past which their delicate offspring must travel in convoy lest they meet the rough kids of the nether regions. The latter in turn regarded those well-dressed children as stuck-up snobs, called them 'little shites with sugar on'. They were considered fair game for ambush. They were all securely locked into a scheme of reference groups as rigid as ethnic stereotypes, derived from and maintained by parental attitudes.

In fairness, the children of the Hollow had to run a more insidious gauntlet than their better-off peers. To make contact with the city proper, even to do their shopping (penny bars in Keeleys of Rathgar, gur cakes in Penelope's cake shop), to go to Mass or to school they had to pass through the daunting stretch of Orwell Road with its large houses and discreet gardens.

Here the business people as well as the higher civil servants, the managers and well-to-do of a poor society lived. These were the national bourgeoisie: Protestants for whom the setting up of the independent state was a catastrophe, but not irredeemable; gombeen Catholics who saw their opportunity and seized it with both hands ...

To travel the Orwell Road four times a day was to be constantly reminded that some people lived at least genteel if not well-padded lives. They saw babies in perambulators (not prams) being wheeled by nursemaids, no less. From behind high walls and privet hedges they heard well-groomed murmurs.

As they streeled to school in the mornings they would be

overtaken by purposeful men in good suits carrying umbrellas and briefcases, striding to catch the tram in Rathgar. A few had cars. There were even some chauffeurs with peaked caps, cranky minions who were obsequious to their employers and proportionately savage towards kids who dared touch their polished chariots. These were people you would read about in comics or books or even see in the pictures: people who always looked washed – even behind their ears – and who always wore their Sunday clothes. Even their kids never got dirty. The kids were the real mystery. Normal kids looked clean for an hour or two on Sunday morning thanks to the previous night's bath but the Orwell Road kids were unforgivably clean every day. The adults were different too. They never said 'hiya' to anybody. They looked the kind of people who wore underpants and might even wear pyjamas instead of their shirts in bed.

It was easy to understand Protestants being clean. That was the difference between them and Catholics: school uniforms and clear complexions. The few Protestants in the Hollow, physically indistinguishable from Catholics, were the exceptions that proved the rule. But if you were confused you could give a simple test: 'Which is better, the lick of a cat or the prod of a pin?' If they answered the former they were Catholic, if the latter, a Protestant.

But all the people on the Orwell Road, whatever their religion, were clean and well-dressed all the time. Some of them attended neither mass nor protestant service, just like the pictures where people never went to the lavatory either and certainly didn't fart or pick their noses.

You might even see the toffs mowing their lawns in the middle of the week when normal fathers were at work, or worse, on Sundays when it was a mortal sin to do unnecessary servile work. Remember that thou keep holy the Sabbath Day; remember the man in the moon? Put there for gathering sticks on a Sunday. Real people spent Sunday walking their children to Mass, walking them home to Sunday dinner and afterwards taking them for a spin on the bikes, a walk by the Dodder or even a bus ride to the museum. You never saw Orwell Road mothers traipsing along, weighted down with shopping bags and fallen wombs, stopping every few yards on the pretext of gossiping but really for a rest. You were more likely to see Orwell Road mothers wearing gloves in their gardens and pruning the roses or hoeing nonexistent weeds.

Their groceries were delivered by cocky young messenger boys with special bikes which they rode with their hands in their pockets. Parents warned about ending up in such dead-end jobs if they didn't do their eckers (homework) and study properly. But this was regarded as the usual adult nonsense that was contradicted by experience. If the arrogant confidence of messenger boys, their cheerful whistling, their casual entree to big houses was the reward for ignorance, who needed school? When these freewheeling souls whizzed confidently through the big gates and up the driveways they were greeted by girls in maids' uniforms. Those unfortunate ill-educated boys had personal contact with lives beyond the experience of the children of the Hollow.

But life was like that. Fortunately they were taught that thou shalt not covet thy neighbour's goods. Be thankful for what you've got. Resentment was expressed through the safety valve of calling names: Stuck Up Snob. Baldy Oul' Toff. Snotty Oliver and his bulldozer.

If that wasn't enough they could exorcise any latent resentment and test the gauntlet by travelling the entire distance from Rathgar to the Hollow without touching the road, through the gardens of the big houses – Stratford, Gainsborough, The Gables, Woodlands, Marianella, Abbotsford and the rest. Dominic nearly made it all the way once but was foiled, not by an irate gardener, but by a large uniformed Garda defecating in the bushes of Stratford which was owned by rich people with a foreign name and fancy accents who were rumoured to own an oil well in Harold's Cross.

The Garda was torn between hastily adjusting his dress and maintaining the dignity of his office which decreed that all movements be slow, deliberate and ponderous. He and the small boy eyed each other in loathing and terror respectively.

Dominic backed away, turned and fled, agonising over whether he should have reassured the man that his secret was safe, that he, Dominic, was no squealer. He refused to go to school next day for fear he would be caught and put in prison. Forever afterwards when he passed a uniform he was on his best behaviour.

The Bethany Home was a place on Orwell Hill to be scurried by if you were on your own. They were told young people were abducted there and forced to change their religion, which meant the death of the soul. So they were taking their souls as well as their lives into their hands if they trespassed there. The big mansion was supposed also to be a home for Protestant orphans from whose bastard ranks Mr Toner claimed all the Number One clerks in Guinness's were recruited. In fact it was a charitable home for unmarried mothers. They exorcised its grimness thus:

'Rollicking Biddy had only one diddy
To feed the bastard on.
The poor little fucker had only one sucker
To grind his teeth upon.'

It ended with a blasphemous leap of logic that nobody ever questioned.

'Tight as a drum, never been done,
Queen of all the virgins.'

But it was still a place of ogres, particularly the matron who was reputed to eat babies alive without salt on them. The unfortunate girls here presumably worked off their sins as profitably for this institution as did their Catholic equivalents slave labour for the convents that doubled as laundries. Sympathy for such wrongdoers was nonexistent. Their condition carried more shame than tuberculosis, which everybody knew was caused by slatternly habits in the home.

Symmetrically placed on the opposing Churchtown Hill was a Catholic convent. The nuns owned a field which would have been perfect for football but was marked with a No Trespassing sign. A boy from Mullingar headed a deputation to seek permission to use the field and was refused. The boy from Mullingar described the head nun as an oul' bitch that was jilted. Ah, the bric-a-brac.

There was a funny bus stop at the top of the Orwell Hill. Dominic shinned up it one day and got a tickling feeling in his genitals. He tried again and found it very pleasant. The third time there was no effect. He told the others and they tried, also without any luck so they said he was either lying or imagining things. Mr Toner was appealed to. He cleared his throat and said it was probably static electricity. Dominic vainly tried it again but the mechanical magic was gone, not to be rediscovered for years ...

The richest family on Orwell Road had a big field behind their house and the children of the Hollow watched longingly as the young scions of this house, not much older than themselves, rode a motorbike round and round, its stuttering sound trailing behind. The Dodder flowed between this field and themselves but they knew in their hearts and souls that much more than a river separated them from such a life. It did not make them envious. Their parents spoke highly of this family: Good Christians, even though they're Quakers. Eventually the family would bequeath half the field as a public park. Such wealth was so remote that the word envy could not convey the silent emptiness they felt when they contemplated it. All that seeped up from the ragbag of their minds was the familiar phrases of parents, teachers and priests: Offer it up. The last shall be first. Blessed are the poor for they shall inherit the kingdom of God. Thou shalt not covet thy neighbour's goods. What cannot be cured must be endured. And so I'm off to Amerikay.

Stray musings did not fill the belly. The main interest was which of the big houses had the best orchard. By general consensus the one near the bridge was tops even though its pears were hard, its apples green and even the crab apples completely inedible. As in the only Bible story they knew (possession of a Bible was out of the question; this dangerous book was only for Protestants and, of course, Bible-thumpers) the desirability of the fruit was in direct proportion to the prohibition and hazards surrounding it.

The main hazard was Frenchie, the owner of the orchard. He was the dead spit of the mad professor in the Buck Rogers follyer-uppers at the Classic, but his nickname came from his black beret, the kind that every cinematic Frenchman wore. The term 'frenchie' was also commonly used for a condom. They only knew things French had some vaguely sordid connotation which was expressed in the doggerel:

'Oh the girls in France
Take their knickers down to dance,
Singing Nelly put your belly close to mine.'

This racial association with things of the flesh was confirmed by the girls who reported that they often saw Frenchie standing at his front window holding his weewee man in his hand and staring shamelessly out at them as they passed. The boys used sing:

'My friend Billy has a tenfoot willie,
He showed it to the girl next door.
She thought it was a snake and hit it with a rake
And now it's only two foot four.'

It added a righteous dimension, a sense of meting out just punishment when they indulged their covetous feelings towards Frenchie's fruit trees.

The orchard was Frenchie's pride and joy. He also had a daughter of uncertain age who helped him keep it in order.

'Boxing the fox' was the term for robbing an orchard. This was not a solo job; it required three thieves in tandem, one for climbing, one for gathering, one for lookout. On this occasion the team was Bern, Joe and Ginty Scully, a seasoned campaigner.

Frenchie was of an age – and probable sinfulness – that regarded attendance at daily Mass as a necessary insurance. The boys were familiar with this habit, if not the reason behind it. One morning in summer, exuding the innocence of children on holiday, the three thieves engaged in a spitting contest at a spot on the river from where they had a good view of his door. They were unconcerned about the daughter. It was a well-known fact that women couldn't run.

Normally they would be splashing in the waters below, diving for the tin cans that gleamed like gold in the brown water. But this was a working day.

Frenchie emerged on schedule, carefully closed his gate and turned towards Rathgar. The thieves moved nonchalantly down the river path which skirted the back garden. They burst into action at the orchard wall. The obstacle of broken glass cemented into the top of the wall was easily overcome, especially when age had rounded most of the sharp edges. Joe and Ginty were given a bunt up by Bern who in turn made a leap and was hauled up the rest of the way. They assumed the attitude of commandos, well known from the comics, dropped over the wall, tensed, studied the terrain, ready for flight should there be a rustle from the direction of the house. Nothing stirred. Orchards were always quiet as graveyards and just as foreboding.

Bern pulled the bag from under his shirt and he and Ginty set about feverishly filling it with pears from the drooping lower branches. Joe climbed the tree and proceeded to shake the top branches where the elusive ripe ones were. It was a waste of time looking for windfalls in the grass; the worms had always got there before them.

Occasionally they would freeze, rigid as statues, straining their ears, eyes darting about like feeding birds. No alarms. No stir from the house.

They relaxed, began to nibble as they worked, would take a bite from one pear, decide it wasn't quite right, throw it away and try another. On such rare occasions life was bountiful. Joe rested from his labours in the tree and, daring as ever, began to softly sing:

'If I had the wings of a blackbird,
And the dirty big arse of a crow,
I'd fly to the top of an oak tree
And shit on the people below.'

Bern hushed him with an urgent 'Shurrup, you'll give us away.'

Joe shushed and squinted at the waterfall his father had

painted. He'd never be able to draw it from this angle, Joe gloated. He relaxed and thought of past glories and other orchards, like the time he was caught by the oul' bitch Murtagh and dragged up to her house and made sit on a low chair against the wall. He had tried to get rid of the apples in his pockets by slipping them behind him. But they fell on to the skirting and rolled out incriminatingly, whereupon the oul' bitch pounced on them. Oh, that was a mess. Even Mr Lee the policeman couldn't placate her when he was asked to intercede. She was fed up with kids robbing her orchard. She was going to have Joe summonsed.

In a desperate last bid to avoid such shame Mr Toner went up to the house and in the middle of his pleadings – I might as well have been talking to a brick wall, he said later – he noticed music on the piano. So he got her talking about songs and they ended up singing 'Pal of My Cradle Days'. She was placated and dropped the charges. Some things, like diplomacy, the oulfella was good at, Joe conceded.

He could see the old mill house perched on the edge of the waterfall, suffocating in greenery, from which the two oulwans were rescued by firemen last winter when the Dodder burst its banks again. That was great gas. Things like that didn't happen often enough. Funny how the river looked so docile now.

He shifted his gaze to the posh houses on the other bank. A figure moved in one of the top windows. Some lazy divil just getting up and they with half a day's work done. He gaped. The figure was naked. A woman! Oh for a telescope. It was that snotty rip that never let them sunbathe in front of her house. She was stretching at the window.

Joe leaned forward to etch every detail on his mind, to be described precisely to his friends. He paddled the air to secure a better grip, clutched at a nonexistent branch and crashed down through the pear tree.

– Nix! Ginty called urgently.

Bern was torn between fear, anger at such carelessness and a niggling concern that his brother's back might be broken.

Fear triumphed as a figure thundered down from the house.

The daughter of the house screeched towards them like an avenging crow. Bern and Ginty scattered. She glanced at Joe moaning on the ground, decided he was not likely to escape without help and followed the others. She tried to catch them both and like Balaam's ass, ended up with none. Bern reached the top of the wall. Ginty jinxed through the shrubs, mangled the immaculate strawberry beds and created the perfect diversion for Joe to hobble away and be hauled up by Bern.

Meanwhile Ginty was outsprinting the woman. He made it to the wall, leaped, received the stigmata from the broken glass, said 'feck' and slithered back down. He tried again and Bern caught him at the same moment as the woman arrived. There was a tug o'war for Ginty's body which he settled by lashing out with his free foot and catching her on the nose.

Safely on the other side they fled downstream, Joe hobbling, Ginty clutching his wounded palms, Bern ushering them along like a mother duck. They reached the safety of an overhanging bank and treated their wounds with dock leaves. When they had stopped shaking they grinned proudly at each other; this story would make heroes of them and Ginty's wounds would be the evidence for doubting Thomases.

· NINE ·

FOR A FEW DAYS THEY WERE CIRCUMSPECT about passing the house at the bridge, averting their heads in deep conversation about imaginary objects on the other side of the road or, if the front door was open, running past like mad. Gradually the episode receded until a conversation between Granda Hope and their mother reminded them.

– I declare to God Oul' Jimmy Moran is gone soft in the head. He's courting a girl half his age.

Granda Hope was on his Saturday visit. Mrs Toner was catching up on the gossip from her native Churchtown. She raised her head from her sewing.

– Who is she?

– That young one that lives with her father at the bridge. (The one that gave chase in the orchard.)

– She's no spring chicken. But still. You'd think Johnny would have more sense.

– He'd give me ten years and not miss them.

Jimmy was Granda Hope's ancient next-door neighbour. He wore a funny high hat with a rounded top and his adult son, Nick, worked for him at the pigs.

– Nick is out of his mind with worry.

Well, there's no fool like an old fool. But it'll come to nothing. He shouldn't worry.

– I seen them myself of a Sunday evening, dressed up to the nines and him with the eyes of a sick dog.

– Is he fool enough to think it's his beauty she's after?

– Oul' Jimmy still has his first communion money. But he might have met his Waterloo here.

The children became interested in this real-life drama and kept an eye out for the courting couple. They were easy to spot at twilight in the Green Lanes beside Milltown golf course. That was a dangerous place to go because of the gypsies who parked their coloured caravans there and decorated the bushes with wet clothes. But the presence of the lovers nerved the children to penetrate a little way. The old man was stooped but his funny hat gave him the edge in height. When he occasionally dropped behind his girlfriend he would surreptitiously remove it to mop his brow, revealing a completely bald pate. She was a stocky woman in her thirties, what Granda Hope would call 'a fine hoult'. She was all smiles, not like the last time Joe and Bern had seen her. She linked the old man's arm in the manner that meant only one thing:

– You'd think she owned him, the children reported back.

They tried to disrupt this unnatural liaison with a few exploratory catcalls from a safe distance.

– Hey, Oul' Jimmy, does your mother know you're out!

– Go on, give her a goozer.

But the couple ignored them. There was not even the hint of a chase. It must be a real case of love.

Love? Ugh. Could you imagine her letting that dirty oul' yoke kiss her. And who'd want to kiss her anyway? Romantic relationships were straightforward. The fellow must be somebody like Clark Gable and the mot must be good-looking like Veronica Lake. People only got lovey-dovey in films where they could hold hands and cry and all that mush. A few minor details were awkward – like where did babies come from and that sort of thing. From under a cabbage leaf satisfied them only for a limited period when having searched their gardens thoroughly there was not a baby to be seen. A few kids whispered that parents did the same thing as dogs, but that was too horrific an idea and was dismissed. They had seen two dachshunds in the garden of a big house on the Orwell Road, stuck together like Siamese twins. It was a great sight and all the kids trooped up to see it. When they fired stones to frighten the dogs apart it worked, but only partially. The two dogs were still joined at the backside, by what looked like a mutual tail. Finally they tugged free and the children realised the extra 'tail' was nothing of the sort. No, they agreed, parents couldn't do that. In the films, proper mothers and fathers slept in single beds because they could afford to. Their own poor parents had to sleep in double beds.

When they became more suspicious, Dominic's best pal Paddy Murtagh and he made a solemn pact that whoever found out first would tell the other. But when eventually and separately they found out they were so embarrassed and disgusted they never discussed it.

Oh for those days of innocence when Dominic and his brothers used to compete for the proudest example of the condition known as 'getting a horn'. For some reason the younger brother was most successful or maybe least inhibited. He could wave his weewee man in waltz time while he sang:

'I'm Popeye the sailor man
I come from the Isle of Man
The girls are so dirty, they lift up my shirty
And tickle me watering can.'

He could also, without touching it, let it relax, then shout 'attention' and cause it to stand vertically. That there might be some remote connection between romance and such innocent games never occurred to them.

They used go for walks on Sunday evening with their father up by the Narrows in Churchtown, which were six-foot wide lanes bordered by immense walls. He said they were built to keep the Irish off the property of the landlords. The lanes were claustrophobic. They occasionally passed Oul' Jimmy and his beloved. Mr Toner would tip his hat as he passed them and continue lecturing his children on the history of the Bottle Tower which was built at the same time as the Narrows and after which the Bottle Tower pub was named. It was built to give employment during the famine. It was difficult to maintain attention to their father's history lectures.

– Not the pub, you fool. The tower. Listen and learn. It's what's called a folly.
– What's a folly?
– Foolishness. Now, what I said was …

Oh yes. Just like Oul' Jimmy's antics, which were confirmed when the girls dashed in one evening with the news that the woman was wearing a ring that would choke an elephant. They would notice such things. Their Granda was morose the following Saturday.

– What's Nick going to do now? As God is my judge if that woman comes into the house it'll be the road for him. And he working for nothing but expectations all these years.

Mrs Toner shook her head and tut-tutted.

– Would nobody talk sense to Johnny?

– He'd listen to nobody. I declare to God. What business has an oul' fella with a young wan like that?

Even the children knew there was a proper age for romance and marriage and all that stuff. They tried to imagine old Jimmy kissing the woman and couldn't. Even their parents didn't make fools of themselves like that.

The matter was dismissed as too absurd until one Saturday when their Granda came in with a beam on his face and the usual 'God save all here.' They caught the note of interest in Mrs Toner's voice.

– You look like the cat got the cream. What ails you?

– Take your ease. All in God's good time. Ah, them childher are getting as big as a house.

They watched him carefully pour his stout. He always left a drop at the bottom of the bottle because of the sediment where slugs lurked. The pubs bottled their own and if the yard boys didn't wash the bottles thoroughly God knows what might creep into them. Snails and slugs have a taste for stout too, you know. He always took one deep draught, stood the bottle and glass carefully on the table and expelled a great gasp of air.

– Ah, God is good.

– Well?

– Well what?

– Any news.

– Only what I heard in the Bottle Tower just now.

– I knew it wasn't the weather had you in fine form.

– Don't be giving out to an old man. Is it my fault that Nick Moran wanted to buy the bar for me?

91

– You could have a bit of will power.

– Indeed and I have will power. He said, 'You'll have a bottle of stout,' and I said, 'I will, certainly I will.' He laughed himself into an endless coughing and wheezing.

– I thought as much. Go out and play, you kids.

They left as slowly as children can, lingering outside the open door to hear every detail, then drifting back in like animate bits of furniture. Granda Hope was more expansive than usual.

– I should be given a medal!

– Wonders will never cease. You told him he was doing Nick wrong?

– Will you take your hour. That's not the way to approach these matters. You have to be circumspectual. I knew in my heart and soul that he was just like any man and would have second thoughts as soon as he put the ring on her finger.

Mrs Toner pouted a little.

– Is that so?

– It is. All I had to do was wait. And I did. As soon as he came and asked could he have a word with me I knew he was having his doubts.

– Go on.

– What do ye think, says he?

– About what, says I?

– You know damn well what, says he.

– I do, says I, and if you want to know what I think, I'll tell you. You're the laughing stock of Churchtown.

– You didn't.

– I did. It was no time for pussyfooting. Straight to the chin.

– What did he say to that?

Granda Hope took a long slurp.

– That didn't bother him at all. They're only jealous, says he.

– Would you credit that! He must be as vain as a peacock.

– Pride comes before a fall.

– Will you get on with it. What was bothering him, then?

– I'll have to get rid of the pigs, says he.

– The pigs!

– That was all that ailed him. She can't stand pigs. It was to be him or the pigs.

– The cheek! What would he live on? What would Nick do?

– No bother to Oul' Jimmy. He still has his first communion money.

– He's a mean old get. Go on.

– I knew on the instant he was putty in my hands. I looked him straight in the eye and said, quiet, mind you, 'What about my pigs?'

Mrs Toner was impatient.

– What have your pigs got to do with it?

Granda Hope hooted and slammed a fist on the table, making his stout shiver.

– That's exactly what he said.

He steadied his glass.

– Oh, the shoe was on the other foot now. What about them, says he? Well, says I, it's not as if she'll be able to avoid the sight or smell of them over the fence. Am I to get rid of mine, too? That rocked him, I can tell you.

– That was perfectly right to say.

– But listen to this. There's no chance of that, I suppose, he says.

– The nerve!

– Didn't I tell you the man thinks of nobody but himself. Ah but I wasn't finished with him. It looks to me, says I, as if you'll have to buy her a new house well away from the avenue and the pigs. Maybe that would satisfy her. That made him think because in his heart he's a mane divil. Bad enough to have to buy a ring, but to buy a house, not to mention leaving the place he was born in, the house he should be preparing to be carried out of at his age.

– Well? What did he have to say to that?

– She'll have me for breach of promise, he says.

Granda Hope had another fit of wheezing laughter. Mrs Toner shook her head disapprovingly.

– And she would too. Some young ones are like that. It's what they can get out of a man.

– Well that's the fix he's in now. He's stuck. But there's one thing I'm sure of: come hell or high water he won't be dragged to the altar. Not with that one, anyway. Nick just told me he's not setting any date for the wedding

– She'll bleed him dry.

But she didn't. They heard the rest of the story weeks later. Oul' Jimmy was leaving Frenchie's daughter home one evening and as was their custom they stopped on the bridge to admire the moon in the water. Oul' Jimmy asked to look at the ring because he'd heard the jewellers who sold it to him had just been arrested. He was afraid it might be watered-down gold. He held it up to the moonlight to get a good luck. Then he stumbled and dropped it over the parapet.

– I declare to God!

They were all as impressed as their mother. Their Granda was in fine fettle.

– Isn't he the cute wan? Mind you, it was me said he'd have to get rid of the evidence. Sure now it's only her word against his and what judge in his right mind would believe a young woman would be attracted to Oul' Jimmy? It'd be against nature.

Granda Hope paused and mused.

– Of course it nearly broke his heart.

– Was he that fond of her?

– Are you mad, girl! Not her! The ring. Ten pounds it cost him.

For days afterwards every child in the Hollow who could swim became a pearl-diver under the bridge. But the ring was never found.

· TEN ·

ROMANCE AND SEX WERE SUCH MYSTERIES that little thought was given to them until one reached a certain age. It was enough to know that girls were different, but in a nonsexual way. They were educated in different classrooms, were squealers and whingers and telltales, had snotty noses and couldn't take a joke.

Fathers and mothers were different but only because of their clear-cut and completely separate roles. There was nothing sexual about it and certainly nothing romantic. These clear categories were only confused slightly by Lady Wogan who lived in a big house in Rathgar.

It may not have been her real name but it suited her because she walked with her sharp little nose stuck in the air. In fact they couldn't make out if she was a man or a woman because she always wore a man's cap, plusfours and leggings and had a voice like a rusty razor blade. If it wasn't for the shopping basket and the mincing walk they would have been completely baffled as to her sex.

The way Lady Wogan strutted and her peaky nose reminded them of one of Granny Hope's hens, the cock that laid an egg. Their Granny always talked with a note of indignation in her voice, no matter what the topic, but when she got going on the cock that laid an egg her voice shifted into higher gear.

– I'd bought a dozen day-old chicks and a cock because we ate the old one at Easter. I declare to heaven when I went down the first morning hadn't he laid an egg.

The children were all ears and queries.

– How did you know it was the cock that laid it?

– Wasn't he sitting on it! What do you take me for?

Granda nodded approvingly.

– That old woman knows hens inside out. Did you ever hear tell of the time ...

– Dry up, you old fool, and let me tell the story.

– Don't be giving out to an old man.

– Anyway, I waited until that eggman called and I asked him what kind of an eejit did he think I was, trying to pass a cock off on me as a pullet. And do you know what that robber said to me?

– What did he say to you?

– He said maybe it was a himopperidite.

– I ask you!

– A what?

– A bloody himopperidite, that's what.

The children pricked up their ears.

– What's a ... what's a ... what's that?

– Now don't get me going.

– But what is it?

– How would I know except it's a cock that lays eggs.

– Why shouldn't a cock lay eggs?

– Because it's a he, not a she.

– Can a hen be a himopper ... whatever it is?

– Would you not be bothering me with your questions.

– But what's the difference?

Like terriers they pursued her, knowing how easily she could be incited to indiscretion. Bern, of course, led the chase.

– What do you mean? What is it anyway?

– What's what?

– A whatchamaycallit. A himopper...

– Child o' grace, leave me alone. I told you once and I'll not tell you again. A himopperidite.

– Why wasn't it called a *her*-opperidite?

– Maybe it should.

– 'Cause maybe the cock was a hen.

– Isn't that what I'm after telling you.

– Then how could it be a *him*-opperidite?

She drew a breath, looked at them impatiently and said:

– Ah, ask me arse.

Success! That was what they had sought. They scuttled out in great glee, conscious of their mother trying to keep a straight face, their Granda whooping with glee, their Granny feigning disgust, their father expressionless. Coarse language was never openly used in the house so it was a relief to hear somebody lapsing into vulgarity. Their Granny and Granda could always be relied on. Once they heard the old man having an argument with Nick Moran and finishing it off with a scornful: 'Would you go and suck me diddy.' It became a favourite weapon in their arsenal of abuse.

Maybe that's why Mr Toner did not seem to approve of them.

He used few expletives and those quite mild: guttersnipe, bowsy, gouger, trollop. Occasionally he would say 'feck it' or 'a pain in me ah'. His children could have expanded his vocabulary with bollix, cunt, gee and the rest of the normal everyday speech they heard, but they valued their lives too much. Imagine if he heard them singing:

'Arsehole, arsehole, arsoldier I will be,
To pis, to pis, two pistols on my knee,
To fight for a cunt, to fight for a cunt,
To fight for a cunt-er-eee.'

Mr Toner of course overheard them and asked despairingly what kind of guttersnipes was he rearing. But he had only himself to blame. Wasn't it he told them about Sweeney Todd, the Demon Barber of Fleet Street, who killed the woman with his razor by giving her arsenic! They didn't get that for a while.

The usual place for learning and exchanging poems that would never find their way into the *Golden Treasury* of verse was the door of the Fever House. It was a good place to shelter from the rain if you couldn't bear to be indoors or, more likely, if a parent told you to get out of their sight, I can't move with you kids under my feet. You were sure to be brought up to date on the latest joke or piece of doggerel, to swop and memorise immortal lines like:

'In the street of a thousand arseholes,
By the light of a swinging tit,
There lives a Chinese merchant,
By the name of Hoo Flung Shit.'

But these crudities were harmless, particularly when they knew they could be easily wiped out with the magic formula: Bless me, Father, for I have sinned, it's a week since my last confession. They were also useful because you didn't have to make up stupid sins like 'I stole the sugar' or 'I was rude to my mother' and so on.

Then they were free to rush out from the dark confessional and recite them all again if they wanted. But they usually restrained themselves until after they had been to the altar on Sunday and received Holy Communion. This was a wafer specially made by the holy nuns and was sacred although it tasted exactly like the wafer from an ice-cream.

Even when the priest wagged it around and genuflected and whispered over it and turned it into God and broke it and ate a bit and then distributed it, the taste still reminded them of ice-cream. Funny too that there was so much to go round. They supposed it was like the miracle of the loaves and fishes.

It stuck to the roof of the mouth, too, because you were forbidden to touch it with your teeth. After all, it was the body and blood of your Saviour and you could only gently lever it with your tongue, gathering lots of spit to wash it down when you finally dislodged it.

– Is that any way to talk about the Blessed Eucharist! Mrs Toner remonstrated. Would you have some respect for your Holy Religion.

In fairness, they had been warned about excess scruples in the story about the boy who had vomited on his way down the aisle after receiving communion. All his breakfast came up and there was God lying in the middle of the mess on the floor. It was left smelling there until Mass was over and everybody had gone. Then, according to the nun, another overzealous boy returned and licked it all up. Yuk. He must have ended up a saint or a madman.

It was a double-edged parable. The boy had overdone it of course, said the nun. And God, being God, had got out in time. But such Faith, children, such Faith.

Apart from the homely Protestants in the Hollow, their

separated brethren as the priest called them, they were all good Catholics. All except the atheist. The atheist parked his dirty big lorry outside their front door. He was entitled to because he lived beside them. But the machine spoiled the symmetry of the circle and was out of proportion to this neat little, tidy little street. Even the neighbours murmured resentfully, but as the atheist was a tough-looking man with a foul mouth and close-cropped red hair which earned him the nickname carrot-head, they did not press the point. As they privately reasoned, how can you expect a man with no religion to behave like a Christian? The lorry was used to haul gravel and sand for builders. Its owner did all the necessary servicing and repairs outside his house and so the road and pathway developed a treacherous and ugly veneer of oil and grit. When it rained, instead of 'wipe your feet' their mother had to screech, 'Take them shoes off before you walk on my clean floor.' She was very fussy like that, which was a nuisance for children constantly coming and going.

Despite warnings about staying away from the man, the lure of his machine was too much and the children were like bees around him when he changed the oil, or fixed a puncture or writhed underneath the chassis, cursing all the while. He was a repellent man, particularly in his atheism, but interesting in that it put him in the same league as Old Nick. He had no horns and nobody ever actually heard him saying he didn't believe in God. As well as that he was always saying 'Holy Jasus' which you wouldn't imagine an atheist would do. Only Catholics said that. So he was hard to figure out.

On the other hand, he was always referring to Holy Joes and craw-thumpers and praying minnies and the like and furthermore, never went to Mass or even to a Protestant service, so he had to be an atheist.

They hovered around him, not too close for fear they'd be included in the bolt of lightning which must come sooner or later to strike him down for his badness.

The matter was complicated when he brought home a good-looking woman with black hair. She must be his wife because she had a small son in tow who was very quiet and allowed out to play only occasionally. The children fastened on the boy to see was he an atheist too, but he was useless. He denied he knew anything about the subject. If he did he certainly wasn't giving the game away. But he promised to try and find out. He came back with the useless answer that his father said he was a human being and that was good enough for anybody.

The question was answered one Sunday when the black-haired woman, Mrs Atheist, brought the boy to the Methodist church in Rathgar. The kids saw them on their own way to Mass. So it was clear he wasn't an atheist but some kind of Protestant which you could do little with except yell proddy-woddy at.

Of course you couldn't do this with somebody you knew like the Tallons or the Jameses or the Woodisons – because you played with them and they weren't like Protestants at all. Protestants were strangers, well-dressed kids from places like Zion Road. In fact, Dominic once met a kid from there who spoke in a posh accent and said his name was 'Rodney Hood – four battleships and a cruiser', showing off that he was English and proud of his association with their great navy, while Dominic was thinking he was lucky to be named after Robin Hood. It just proved the English were thick as well. Still, he had to rack his own brains to think of an equivalent boast about his identity. There was feck all he could think of so he relapsed into his father's explanation: the English stole everything from us and grew fat on our misery.

Anyway, the black-haired woman kept very much to herself. The Toner children often heard her singing through the walls, especially on Saturday mornings. Of all the times to show off that she had a hoover! It caused interference on their radio, just when the omnibus edition of 'Dick Barton Special Agent' was on. It was the only time they could listen to it in peace because the daily episode was interrupted by their father.

– Why are you listening to that English rubbish? Could you not listen to something decent.

It was the same with Radio Luxembourg.

– Switch off that jungle music. Have you no taste? It would give you a headache, all those D.B.'s caterwauling.

D.B. stood for 'Dirty Bitches' who were women who sang jazz, the lowest form of music.

The only time they could listen in peace was on Saturday morning. Why couldn't the woman next door do her hoovering when 'Making and Mending' or 'The Palm Court Orchestra' or the news were on? It didn't make her popular with them. All they could do was turn up the radio full blast and continue smoking the rolled-up brown paper fags, taking turns to keep nikko for their mother coming home from the shopping in Rathgar with the penny toffee bars.

A kind of polite friendship developed between Mrs Toner and the woman next door. From this they learned she was worse than a Protestant; she was a lapsed Catholic 'for whom the pangs of guilt are greater than the flames of hell', which they had learned in school but which their mother turned on them for saying.

– Judge not lest you be judged, she said. That woman would put many a so-called Catholic to shame.

When she added another trimming to the end of the rosary they knew the 'special intention' was for the woman next door. It had to be. It couldn't be Oul' Rock, the cranky man up in one of the fancy houses at the top of the road, who had changed his religion to marry a Protestant with money.

– An apostate, said Mr Toner. His conscience will never give him a minute's peace.

– I thought the twelve apostles were good.

They knew about these from the twelve tiny teaspoons in the kitchen drawer. They had the heads of the bearded apostles carved on them.

– Apostate. Not apostle. Apostate. Do you never listen? Listen and learn.

One evening when the atheist was changing a wheel on his lorry the jack slipped, the axle came down and the wheel rocketed out against his face. They all thought he was dead, but it's hard to kill a bad thing and he only spent a couple of days in hospital. Still, it gave him a terrible scar which exaggerated his scowl and earned him another nickname: 'Scarface', like Al Capone.

Still the lorry fascinated them. They didn't really disobey their parents but you couldn't help passing the lorry and lingering a bit, envying the kids like Larry Hartnett before he went to America to become a cowboy who was allowed to sit in the cab and hand the atheist his tools. Only once had Dominic been in a car and that was when Mr Scully brought Ginty and himself to the Stella cinema where the fountain in front of the curtains changed from red to green just before the film started. It was raining and Ginty ordered his father to put on the windswipers, which he did and Ginty grinned knowingly at Dominic. They drove at forty-five miles an hour down the Rathgar Road, a breathtaking dash which was remembered long after the film was forgotten.

Anyway, this day the kids were playing football in the circle and their ball zoomed towards the lorry and hit the atheist as he emerged from under it. Maybe his face was still sore but he dashed out to give them a piece of his mind. The only one who didn't scatter was Joe who had not been playing football but was trying to set up a world record for bouncing his own ball, using his hand as a racquet. He was close to the record so he ignored the big man shouting at him. Later he said he was paralysed with fright but nobody was going to stop him breaking the record. He had to count out loud so as not to lose score, which the man interpreted as insolence, and his scar glowed red and the other kids were sure Joe was going to get a clatter. But the apparent calmness of Joe won the day and the atheist returned to his lorry growling. Meanwhile Joe missed the ball and naturally blamed it on the atheist's interruption. He muttered 'Scarface' audibly and fled for his life.

The atheist had no chance of catching him so he marched up to the Toner's door to complain. Mrs Toner opened the door and her face assumed its frostiest expression when she saw who it was.

– Your young fella better watch his tongue, missus.

– Is that so?

– It is so. Name-calling is only for gutties.

– What did he say?

– I wouldn't repeat it.

– From what I've heard, that's a change. Now would you mind not putting your feet on my clean step.

He departed with bad grace. She slammed the door loudly only to reopen it a minute later, a basin of water and scrubbing brush in her hands with which she proceeded to scrub the step more vigorously than was necessary. She was in time to let him see her as he walked furiously up his front path next door. The children were awed.

War had been declared. The atheist began to build a high wall between the two back gardens. Higher and higher it rose until it cut off the sunlight from their small vegetable patch. Mr Toner glared helplessly but could do nothing, because the wall was actually in the atheist's garden. The final straw was when he removed the ridge tiles from their adjoining coal sheds and used them for an extension he was building. They were replaced with a crude concrete strip. Mrs Toner was furious at her husband's inaction.

– Are you going to let him get away with it?

Silence.

– Anybody that was half a man would do something.

– I told you I reported it to the Corporation.

– Corporation, my eye. This is private property.

– You can't take the law into your own hands.

– Isn't that what he's done!

– There's a right way and a wrong way to approach these things.

The children were half ashamed and half relieved that Mr Toner wasn't going to take on the atheist. They had witnessed the man in action against Oul' Corcoran down the road and it was a frightening experience. The atheist held a starting handle in his fist and yelled obscenities.

– Go 'way, you yellowbellied little shit.

Mr Corcoran was lucky to have his wife and mother-in-law

to hold him back as he made as if to scramble over his front gate to get at the tormentor.

– Did you hear that foulmouthed get? Let me at him.

– No, Johnny, no. Don't soil your hands on him.

– No, Johnny, no, mimicked the atheist in a falsetto voice.

Corcoran looked as if he'd have a heart attack soon. He rattled the gate like a dog trying to shake off his chain. In the event, the only things exchanged were epithets which caused mothers to haul their youngsters indoors.

They would hate to see their father humiliated like that, or worse. At the same time they were uncomfortable at the implication in their mother's words. Nobody likes to think their father is chicken.

As time passed the atheist seemed to become even more bad-tempered. Soon nobody would even give him the time of day. Mrs Toner said there was a devil in him which would destroy him. Some nights they heard shouting and crying next door. On one of these nights there was a loud knocking on their own door and they were sure it was the atheist come to kill their own father. But it was only his wife with the little boy, asking for God's sake to be let in.

They heard her sobbing in the hallway before she was ushered into the sittingroom. The door was shut firmly. Next morning she and the boy were gone and never reappeared in the Hollow.

Months later the Toner children were sent off on the bus to attend the boy's birthday party in a tiny flat off the South Circular Road where all the Jews lived. They knew this because they were told that Jewish children used go to the local school which was Catholic until the other kids started baptising them in the lavatories and that was the end of that.

They were the only children at the party and it wasn't much fun. When they sang 'Happy Birthday', Mrs Atheist looked as if she was going to cry but she pulled herself together and gave them crackers to pull. They left in time to catch the 47A bus at Kelly's Corner, their pockets stuffed with sweets and biscuits which made the party seem not bad after all. That was the last any of them saw of Mrs Atheist and her human being son.

Meanwhile the atheist had taken on a housekeeper, or so their mother carefully described the girl. They only caught glimpses of her hanging out the clothes and then she too was gone in exactly the same circumstances: a late-night knocking on the door and a hysterical girl looking for sanctuary. The children tiptoed from their beds to the landing and huddled there, straining to catch the murmurs from below. They were thrilled to hear the word gun mentioned and the girl sobbing that she was a respectable girl. The sittingroom door was again firmly closed. But they had heard enough.

They knew about these things. Hadn't their mother pointed out a window in a house in Stephen's Green which had the mark of a rosary beads on it every Good Friday? She told them that years before a maid in the house had rejected her employer's advances and tried to protect herself with her rosary beads. The brute flung the beads through the window. No matter how often the glass was replaced, the mark of the beads reappeared as a sign of God's anger at him.

In whispers they speculated on what might have happened next door. They froze when they heard their father emerge from the room and leave through the back door of the house. They were thrilled that he might be going to take on the bad guy next door, just like in the pictures. As Mr Toner was obviously the 'chap', they had no fears for him even if the atheist had a gun; the chap never gets killed in the pictures. Also, it was a way of expiating his cowardice over the roof tiles. The chap always does that: puts up with insults and the lot until finally he buckles on his gun which he has sworn on his mother's grave never to use again and goes out in the hot sun to confront the bad guy and his henchmen skulking on the roofs. It was a bit of a letdown when they heard that he had only gone up the road for Mr Barry the policeman.

Next day the girl was gone and so was the atheist. There was great excitement when somebody said he was gone to prison for life in the Black Maria. He was interesting enough as an atheist, but to be living right next door to a real criminal was a great distinction.

It was only wishful thinking. They were disgusted when the man reappeared a few days later and carried on as if nothing had occurred.

Was the cinema the only place where real criminals existed?

· ELEVEN ·

THE SANCTIONS WERE NOW RUTHLESSLY ENFORCED on the Toner children. It was heartbreaking for them to see other kids climbing on the lorry and conversing intimately with the atheist as he worked underneath. They had to walk by as if that huge and fascinating piece of machinery, which nearly blocked the narrow road, didn't exist. So the man was an atheist. So he was a dirty old man with a foul mouth. What had morality got to do with mechanics?

The sanctions lasted until the day the lorry brought a load of turf to a house across the road and as usual the other kids swarmed around it. The temptation was too much for Dominic. Reasoning that his business was with the turf, not with the owner of the lorry, and that he had a perfect right to engage in some honest and lucrative toil, he joined in the fray with the expectation of a few coppers. It was unlikely that the atheist would identify him amongst the milling kids so he clambered up on the lorry.

Much later his mother said that God had punished him for disobedience. When the lorry was empty and only the brown dust remained, Dominic jumped off. Unfortunately the back of his jersey snagged on a rough edge and he was suspended in midair. He turned to free himself just as the thin material gave way. He fell, his elbow colliding with the edge of the pavement. Standing up quickly he felt no pain but his left arm dangled strangely like a puppet's arm that has lost its string. It frightened him so he clutched it in his other arm and ran across the Circle to his own house. That was his real undoing for, as he learned in the weeks he spent in hospital, a sharpened bone of his shattered elbow sliced through the main artery in his arm.

Meantime he wasn't sure what was wrong but it must be serious because his mother fussed over him without any abuse and he could see all the kids crowding outside the livingroom window to see if he was alive or dead. Mrs O'Neill and Mrs Murtagh came in and made tea and tsk-tsked about that antichrist and his lorry and why he should have been left to rot in jail. There was shaking of heads and pursed lips and 'Does it hurt, love?' and Dominic never had such attention in his life. He was made to sit absolutely still with his arm in a sling made from one of his mother's nylon stockings.

He was brought to the Meath Hospital in Mr Coyne's hackney cab, the same one he had run into with his Granda's cart. The other kids crowded around enviously and he grinned at them, waving with his good arm as the car pulled away.

He enjoyed the hospital, once he got over the fright of the big room with huge lights and people dressed in green looking down at him. They tried to suffocate him with chloroform and had the cheek to ask him to breathe deeply. He held his breath as long as he could but they got him eventually and he died. He woke up sitting peaceably on the front lawn of the Presentation Convent in Terenure, his first school, looking at the red brick walls and the leprechauns that surrounded him, smiling agreeably. He could hear a swishing sound and realised it was the grass growing. The leprechauns were just sitting there like statues so he relaxed and enjoyed the sound which was like a giant breathing in and out. It was a pleasant death and when he came back to life his mother was there holding a bowl for him to get sick in.

She visited him every day, wearing the shiny black hat, always bringing him biscuits and once even a banana. She treated him as lovingly as she had when he was the baby, years ago. He didn't know why she looked so worried because it was great having a bed to himself for once and he was the pet of the ward which was full of men. He heard the doctor saying 'gangrene' to her once. He assumed it meant the people in green clothes in the brightly lit room to which they brought him once more and where he once again heard the grass growing. Mrs Toner told him about the cut vein in his arm, which didn't make sense because he could see no blood. In fact it was the cleanest accident he had ever had.

He learned to read in hospital. The chart over his head with the zigzag lines had his name and religion written upside down on it and he had to look at it so often that he eventually made out what it meant. The nurse explained the zigzag lines to which she added a bit every time she put the thermometer in his mouth. He was terrified he'd bite through it and die like the fellow in the *Fu Manchu* film who was given ground glass in his sandwich and died roaring.

He had a bed in the men's ward because the children's section had no room. They were nice to him but they all carried containers like soda siphons with rubber tubes which vanished into their pyjamas. He was shocked when he realised their mickeys weren't working properly. That's why they had tubes. And the liquid was pee. It was his big dread, the day they were going to give him one too. Oh God, why had he got up on that lorry? Even his mother's assurances were no good. Everybody in the ward had one, which meant he'd get one too. 'No,' she said, 'that's not what's wrong with you.' He was mistrustful still. Even if she wasn't lying, supposing the nurse made a mistake, thought there was something wrong with his mickey and tied a tube and bottle to him. How would he go to school like that?

The day his mother met the doctor halfway up the ward, he was sure she was giving permission to apply a tube and bottle to him. That's maybe why she started to cry when she kissed him. He could stand anything but her bawling.

– It's okay, he said. They can do what they like.

– They're not going to do anything to you.

– Honest?

– Honest. Although you nearly lost it.

He shivered.

– If the gangrene hadn't stopped they would have had to take it off from the elbow.

– Me elbow? They're not going to give me a bottle, then?

– Don't be silly. You're the luckiest boy alive.

– How did it stop?

– Because I stormed heaven, that's why. We all did. The whole Hollow was praying for you.

But he knew it was her and the novena. Every Monday night she walked all the way to the copper-domed church in Rathmines for the Novena of the Miraculous Medal. You only had to do it for nine Mondays to get anything you wanted, but she was doing it for years and never missed a week. When the priest in the Church of the Three Patrons on Rathgar Road saw the great business Rathmines was doing he started it himself and she transferred her custom because it was nearer. She tried to get them all to do it and often they were unlucky enough to be around when she was going so they knew the whole rigmarole, the hymns, the rosary, the litany which they used answer: 'Spray for Uh, spray for uh', instead of 'Pray for us,' because it relieved the monotony.

> 'He gazed on thy soul, it was sinless and rare,
> Hail full of grace, we devoutly declare
> Conceived without sin, thine own childhood a or b (they could never make that word out)
> Oh spray for uh, who have recourse to thee.
> Sweet star of the sea,
> Sweet star of the sea, Oh spray for uh etcetera.'

The devotions seemed to go on for hours and then there was benediction which was interesting because the altar boy who swung the thing with incense in it was always letting the fire go out and had to bring it over to the priest to light it again. Then he'd swing it again for a while like a pendulum until it went out again. What an eejit. If they'd had that job they'd show him how. They'd swing it over their heads so that you'd see the flames. But the eejit who held it was timid. Eventually after bringing it to the priest to relight it a couple of times he was sent off the altar in disgrace.

After that there was only the Stations of the Cross to look at. The 'Jesus Meets His Most Afflicted Mother' one was ridiculous. There the poor divil was, blood coming out of everywhere including his head with the crown of thorns, not to mention the big cross he had to hump along, and they were expected to feel sorry for his whinging oulwan?

Bern passed the time by speculating on the ambulatory that ran all the way round the church, even the back of the altar. It would make a great race track. But no matter how inventive the daydreaming, you were always left staring at a picture or a sign carved into white marble like: 'I have loved the beauty of thy house, O Lord, and the place where thy glory dwelleth;' or 'This statue erected through the generosity of ...' There were a lot of them. No wonder priests had plenty of money.

He had been in the hospital six weeks and his brothers and sisters were not let in to visit him. No children were allowed in because unruly kids might disrupt the ordered world of the holy nuns who ran the place. Or it might be to stop them catching the pox or something, you never knew. You could be sure there was some good reason. That's the way the world was.

Anyway, when he got home it was all the better. They treated him with relative deference, didn't even mind when he got cream crackers and they only got bread. His legs were very shaky but he didn't have to go to school yet. All in all, it was the best time of his life. And one day as he was passing the atheist, the man spoke gruffly but kindly to him, which shocked Dominic because he thought he'd be given out to for being on the lorry. Dominic mumbled something and the man pressed a half-crown into his hand. He couldn't be all that bad.

Nevertheless when a gravel pit collapsed on the man shortly afterwards there was an unspoken agreement that it was a judgement, particularly as they said he was in a single embrace with a woman. A single embrace? What's so special about that? Never you mind. Everything is subject to the will of God. Their mother added one grudging prayer to the rosary but they doubted if it was enough to save the man from hell. Eventually it emerged that it was not a single embrace, but a sinful embrace.

– What? What's a sinful embrace? What's the difference?

– Don't be inquisitive.
– But what is it?
– Never mind.
They were still as mystified.

It was strange with all these prayers floating up to heaven like smoke, directed straight at God, that life should be so constantly punctuated by accidents which seemed to defeat their very purpose – to deliver us from evil, amen. How such an appeased, praised, glorified and generally spoiled oul' fella with a beard who was supposed to be omnipotent could allow these things to happen was a puzzle until they realised it was a mystery. That removed the matter happily beyond their attempts at comprehension. This was the only good thing about religion; you didn't have to work things out.

Also, you got new clothes for first communion and confirmation. The boys were cheated a bit on that though. Their father made them wear an Irish costume for their first communion. It had a black jacket with a kind of orange cloak pinned to the shoulder with a Tara brooch. It was made by Mrs Toner for Bern to appear in a concert and the parents decided it would be a shame to waste it on one outing so the eldest boys were made to wear it on these religious occasions. Worst of all they had to put on a saffron kilt, of all things. They were so sensitive about it that anybody who looked sideways at them was liable to get a dig in the snot. They couldn't wait to get home and put on the real new clothes.

When it was the turn of the young Johnny, he rebelled and refused to wear it on the grounds that it had been worn out by his older three brothers. He was the baby and could get away with anything. And by then Mr Toner seemed to have given up turning them into patriots. He was also getting very deaf so he couldn't argue very well, particularly with Mrs Toner when she defended young Johnny's right not to wear girls' clothes for his communion.

– It was all very well years ago, but youngsters nowadays are all in the fashion. I tell you, it's his first communion or the Irish costume.

His first communion won. They envied Johnny and felt it served him right when he had his accident. They heard about it from Kitty who worked in the sweet kiosk at the bridge.

– Is your little brother all right?

– What's wrong with him?

– I don't know. One of the kids came up and said Johnny Toner broke his bum.

– What?

– That's what he said. Said he was gushing blood.

Young Johnny had been sliding down a grassy incline when a piece of rusty tin embedded in the soil sliced through his buttock. He ran home, highly embarrassed, to inspect the wound in the bathroom mirror. He had two worries: one, would he have to bare his bottom to strange people; two, would he get lockjaw. This was the terrible fate which resulted from a dirty cut, particularly if it was between the index finger and the thumb. How such a wound could cause your mouth to shut tight and never open again was beyond him, but it was a fact. Mr Toner said so. Suppose this present wound had the same effect on his backside? He shook as he tried to staunch the blood with toilet paper – actually newspapers cut up in small squares – but it was no use so he braced himself to tell his mother.

She looked at it in horror and hustled him off to a doctor. Johnny had to eat his meals standing up for a few days but nobody mocked him. The thought of what might have been made them shiver.

The passing of time was calibrated with such accidents. A period would be recalled by reckoning it as before or after the time Joe dislocated his wrist trying to do pull ups on a branch which gave way, or Dominic's arm, or Laura's scarlet fever when the Corporation came and sprayed all the mattresses, or the baby's pram running away down Orwell Hill with the baby in it, or old Mr Gullman being hit on the head by Bern's improvised throwing hammer, or the fork of Mr Toner's bike collapsing on the Harold's Cross bridge and him missing death under the wheels of a car, or Bern catching the key of his train in his rectum, or Nancy swallowing a pin.

Nancy's pin was memorable because they were introduced to their Granny's strong opinion that nature was the best healer. She refused to go to doctors. 'Quacks all of them. Only in it for the money. They cure one disease and cause another. Leave it to nature.' She and Granda Hope lived until they were ninety and eighty-four respectively, so she can't have been far wrong.

Nancy's pin was a classic example. She swallowed it on the way home from school because she was daydreaming. Nancy was always a bit of a daydreamer. One Sunday she was at Mass and woke up to hear clapping at the end of the priest's usual boring sermon. She wondered what kind of eejit would clap in church and when she looked down found it was herself. She never heard the end of that.

She was daydreaming this time because she had picked the pin up and that was a sign of luck. Unfortunately she had her last sweet in the other hand and when somebody asked her for it she said she had none left and popped the contents of her hand into her mouth. The wrong hand, of course. The hand with the pin. What a dope.

The good news was that it was a safety pin and it was closed. It served her right for being so mean, her companions said, but they were uncomfortable at the thought of the pin moving down her gullet and suddenly springing open and sticking in God knows where, maybe even in the thirty-foot tube that their father said was in the stomach. It would be like trying to get a hook out of an eel's mouth, said somebody, and they all knew what a mess that was. You always had to cut off its head.

Nancy was rushed to hospital and they imagined her being cut open and searched. But she blithely arrived home the following day, head intact, saying they hadn't touched her, except to give her cotton-wool sandwiches which brought the pin out on its own.

– How?
– It just came out.
– But how?

– I told you.

– But how? Did you vomit it out?

– Don't be stupid.

– How, then?

– Ask no questions and you'll be told no lies.

– Go on. Tell us.

– Don't be nosey.

They pressed her for more details but she refused to discuss the matter. They called her a cranky rip and ignored her. Served her right if the cure was so embarrassing that she couldn't brag about it.

Apart from references in dirty jokes and rhymes, the private functions and parts of the body were absolutely taboo. They existed all right, but in some unmentionable limbo of disapproval. It built up to such a curiosity that Dominic once lay sick in bed, carefully arranging the covers so that he was partially and indecently exposed to the view of a casual passerby whom he hoped above hope would be Nancy, sent up by his mother to deliver an egg-flip or gruel. Surely she would exchange looks with him. She must be as curious as he. They could maybe touch each other. At least talk. But when Nancy came up she took one look at him, said, 'You dirty thing', and ran down to tell her mother. There was no use pretending he was asleep. Mrs Toner gave him a lecture and told him to get up out of that bed, you little get, you're not sick at all. In vain he protested he didn't know what she was talking about. He had been fast asleep. It was just Nancy's dirty mind. She ignored him.

– Don't be unnatural, she said. I can't believe a child of mine would do such a thing.

It must have been the knock on the head he got. It happened at the time of a general election. Mr and Mrs Toner went off as usual in the Fianna Fáil car to vote for Mr De Valera, one of the few people they ever heard Mr Toner speak well of. Mrs Toner referred to him as 'The Long Fellow' or 'The Lanky Oul' Get' or 'The Spaniard'. She would never commit herself to saying who she actually voted for and they never knew because she described the Opposition, 'that other crowd' in equally scathing terms. Even though as a young woman at dances she had hidden guns in her dress when the Black and Tans raided the halls, she still defiantly said they had been better off under the British.

They knew that Ireland never produced a Rockfist Rogan or a Biggles or a Dan Dare and the Irish were never heroes in war pictures, so she might be right even if everybody said the British had murdered the Irish for seven hundred years and particularly priests which was worst of all.

The one decent thing seemed to be 1916 but it was a bit of a let down to find their father wasn't in the scrap. 'I was only fourteen,' he protested. Some excuse. Their mother said there were young fellows of twelve acting as messenger boys for Patrick Pearse. So where was he? Probably studying or painting or singing or something boring like that. Later they found out that the nearest he got to the action was Bolands' Mills where the bullets had punctured the sacks of flour and he and his pals went down to fill paper bags and bring the flour back to their mothers.

– Was that dangerous?

– You never know. We could have been shot as looters.

That at least was something.

Mrs Toner had no illusions about the leaders of the country.

– They're only feathering their nests. Look at the fur coats on their wives. Those ones never had a ration book.

– God give me patience.

– They wouldn't know the price of a loaf of bread.

– Will you have sense. If it wasn't for them Blueshirts and West Britons always criticising, always hounding and harassing a man like Dev – a man whose boots they're not fit to wipe – this would be the greatest little country on earth.

– What we need is a dictator.

– Oh typical. Typical. You shouldn't interfere in things you don't understand. We don't deserve a man like De Valera.

– Sure they're all afraid to say boo to him.

– You know nothing about it.

– I know the price of food.

– The Irish are an ungrateful race. He kept us out of the war.

– Hiding behind England's skirts! And starving us into the bargain while he and his buddies were living off the fat of the land.

– We don't deserve our freedom.

But still they went off together in the Fianna Fáil car, leaving the children to listen in peace for once to Dick Barton.

On this particular night a row developed between Joe and Dominic as to who should have the best seat, the one between the radio and the fire. They were trying to push each other off it when Joe gave Dominic a box on the ears and skipped across the room. It was the ruse of an older, cuter operator: lure Dominic across the room after him then use his superior speed to get back to the chair first.

Dominic, always on a short fuse, rose to the bait and charged, head first, the traditional way to attack somebody bigger than oneself. Joe neatly sidestepped. Dominic thundered on and crashed into the corner of the mahogany chair which split his head open.

Laura took charge and sent the others to get help. Mrs Murtagh came and used brown sticky paper to try to hold the wound closed because there was no elastoplast. Dominic sat motionless because he was afraid his brains would spill out with the blood. When Mr and Mrs Toner arrived, they used the election car to bring him to the hospital.

– The only favour that crowd ever did us, said Mrs Toner.

– Hush, woman.

Sixteen stitches were the result. Joe got a ticking off and Fianna Fáil lost the election.

· TWELVE ·

IT WAS HARD TO KNOW WHETHER MR AND MRS TONER LIKED one another. Dominic saw them embrace only once and that was on Christmas morning. He saw it because he and the other kids were doing the ceremonial parade down the stairs with their parents' presents: a packet of hairpins, six razor blades, twenty cigarettes, cheap Woolworths geegaws with sentimental poems to the best mother and father in the world.

Dominic was proud of his present for his mother that year: a bottle of perfume. It had caused him some aggravation and embarrassment. He had brought his single shilling into the chemist's shop in Rathgar, not Hayes Conyngham & Robinson which was for snobs in fur coats, but the small one beside the Monument Creameries. He asked for the handsome perfume box in the window which was priced at exactly one shilling.

When he left the shop he examined his purchase and discovered that the bottle inside was deceitfully tiny. He marched back in and complained so they gave him a bigger bottle, this time without the camouflage of packaging. It was much better value. He left them in no doubt that he knew they had tried to rob him but the girl behind the counter had the brazen nerve to only grin at him.

Coming down the stairs on Christmas morning his older brothers and sisters gave a little cheer and he saw that his parents were embracing in the middle of the diningroom. He deduced they were making up after a cold spell. They never had the kind of rows that floated out the windows of other houses; the shouting and screeching and bad language that made close neighbours adopt a preoccupied demeanour, as if they couldn't hear a thing.

His parents never shouted at one another. They shouted at the kids all right but you only knew they were rowing when there was silence between them. His mother would pedal the sewing machine vehemently, occasionally pausing to sigh, hold up a torn pants, take an endless breath but finally let it out with a 'Tsk, tsk, tsk, God give me patience.' At which his father would rattle the paper noisily, look up to heaven and mutter, 'And me more money.' All other remarks were directed at the kids. At such times they trod warily, fearful of the invisible tripwires.

But that Christmas was all right. It was like what their dead Uncle Tom had told them of the First World War. It was Christmas Eve, he said, and the British Tommies heard voices across no man's land singing 'Silent Night' in German.

– That's *Stille Nacht* in German, Mr Toner interjected.

Uncle Tom continued: carefully the Tommies peeped over the top of the trench and saw the Germans doing the same. Like shy rabbits they all climbed out of their burrows and approached each other through the barbed wire and bomb craters, shook hands and wished each other a happy Christmas.

– And the next day they continued blowing each other's brains out, their father added.

Uncle Tom just stared out the window. Mr Toner pressed the point.

– War is idiotic.

Their own internecine quarrels were suspended in the house for Christmas. There was too much to do, too much to think about, like what they would get as a present, what they would get their parents, would Granny Hope give them their usual half-a-crown and so forth.

They earned money for presents by cleaning the house. They also cut out every newspaper advertisement which featured Santa Claus and saved them to make decorations. They even drew their own Christmas cards which had a star, a candle and a fir tree, all easy to draw once they saw how Bern did it. He was very good at drawing.

Mrs Toner made the pudding weeks before. They all had to stir it which was difficult because the mixture was very heavy. But it was worth it because the wish it entitled them to counted heavily with Santa Claus. Even Mr Toner had to stir it and pour the bottle of stout in.

Then she cooked it and hung it in a cotton cloth on the handle of the back door. It looked like a punch bag. It was just the right height for them to suck at it from below when nobody was looking. They could just about get the taste that way and anticipate its glorious richness on the great day.

As far as the other essential mainstay of Christmas, the turkey, was concerned Mrs Toner took, in their opinion, serious risks. She did nothing about it until Christmas Eve. Then she got the bus into Moore Street with either Bern or Laura as escort. Her theory was that all those robbers of butchers would have panicked by then and would practically pay you to take their turkeys away. She also hinted at the possibility of picking one up in the bus, or in a pub, where a drunk might have left it. But they knew well she was only bragging. She'd never do such a thing.

To their relief she would eventually arrive with the fabulous bird and stories of traipsing from shop to shop and stall to stall until she found the best bargain. They were familiar with Moore Street. Apart from the street-stalls with their raucous owners there was a warren of lanes behind it, like an Arab market. Each with its share of stalls. Whenever they needed new clothes or shoes, as for first communions and special occasions, their mother brought them there and haggled with the owners for the best bargains.

Immediately she arrived with the turkey she would set to cleaning and plucking the bird. The pong was awful when she cut the head and feet off and pulled the guts out of it. They vied for the feet. You could frighten the younger ones by sticking it in their faces and pulling a certain grisly sinew to make it move.

At bedtime the youngest had to carry a lighted candle up the stairs to the landing window to indicate to the Holy Family that if they were stuck they could sleep in the Toner house.

More usefully, it would be a guide for Santy for whom a bottle of stout and a biscuit were left on the diningroom table. In bed they hushed each other so that they wouldn't miss the sound of the bells on his sleigh.

This was the Christmas the older children had clubbed together and bought a secondhand windy-up gramophone and some 78 records. These included John McCormack singing 'Panis Angelicus' at the Eucharistic Congress in 1932. Perhaps it was the music and its sentimental religiosity that made the parents call a truce.

The gramophone featured steel needles which had to be screwed into a heavy arm and clumsy children tended to drop the arm on the records. There was a record of a song called 'Whistling in the Dark' which had a lovesick man being accosted by a copper and explaining: 'It's all right, Officer, I'm, only (sings) Whistling in the dark ... I see the lights all over town, as I go walking up and down, I'm only whistling in the dark....'. But the needle gouged the record and the man repeated eternally: 'It's alright, Officer, I'm only click ... It's alright, Officer, I'm only click ... For obvious reasons, the children found this version much more entertaining.

The 'Panis Angelicus' suffered no accidents but it was played continuously throughout Christmas Day and St Stephen's Day and the rest of the holidays so that it simply wore out. Eventually all you could hear was surface noise and the faint voice of McCormack struggling to be heard. But by that time they all knew the hymn off by heart so it didn't matter. That was the year young Johnny got his first bike.

Dominic had to stay behind that Christmas morning while the others went off to the usual six o'clock mass in Mount Argus. Dominic resented having to babysit his younger brother because the early morning ritual was one of his favourite parts of Christmas. Not the mass itself; that was a bore, apart from the soprano singing 'Adeste Fideles'. But the walk in the dark along the Orwell Road with hardly a sinner abroad was exciting. Mr Toner took his hand when he was the youngest and that itself was pleasing because it happened so rarely.

The kids would kick the wet dead leaves until their mother told them it would ruin their shoes.

– And stop dragging your heels, Mr Toner would call.

Sometimes they would see a dim figure rambling uncertainly on the other side and know it was one of the gentle alcoholics going home. They couldn't understand how anybody could mess up Christmas like that.

One Christmas there was snow so deep that they had to follow their father in Indian file, stepping carefully in his footprints, noting the rubber-tyre pattern of his soles. He made jokes about it being the nearest they'd ever get to following in his footsteps.

On this particular Christmas, Dominic knew that Santy had brought young Johnny a bike. When his young brother woke and bawled for his Mammy the only way Dominic knew to quieten him was to tell him about the surprise. The child was alert, dry-eyed instantly.

– Where is it?

– Downstairs, in the sittingroom.

– I don't believe you.

– Well, don't then.

– I want to see it.

– No. We can't look at the presents before they come home. Anyway Daddy always locks the door.

– Maybe he forgot.

– No chance.

– I want to see it.

Dominic learned the irresistible force of a child's insisting.

– Okay, just one look and then straight back up here. And don't let on you saw it.

– Okay.

They slipped like thieves downstairs and tried the door. It opened. The room was like Aladdin's cave. All the presents were arranged under the tree. Naturally once he had seen the bicycle, young Johnny would not let it go. It was lucky it was raining or he would have taken it out on the road. It had rained for a week and they had been singing 'I'm dreaming of a wet Christmas'. They certainly got it that year.

122

When the others came home from mass, Mrs Toner's face creased in disappointment at seeing Johnny already enjoying the bike. She snapped at Dominic:

– The only thanks I wanted was to see his face when he got it.

She had a way of saying things that made you feel miserable. But she soon cheered up and went off to the kitchen to make a cup of tea to warm them all up. They thought it was their breakfast but she said, 'Not at all, this is Christmas, we'll have a real breakfast later.' And after opening their presents they did: eggs and rashers and white pudding and no rationing on the bread or marmalade.

At midday Granda and Granny Hope arrived in Mr Coyne's hackney cab. No expense was spared at Christmas. The old folks were installed in the sittingroom with a bottle of stout each so that they could survey their adored grandchildren. Mrs Toner greeted them and disappeared back into the kitchen. Mr Toner sat dutifully with the old people and sipped his annual glass of whiskey. Though he worked in a brewery he rarely drank. His entitlement of two free pints a day was given away to fellow workers whom he said drank too much already. It was rumoured among his children that the reason for his down on drink was that his own father, who died when he was eight, was an alcoholic. On Christmas Day he would relent and have a couple of bottles of stout too. Mrs Toner would sip one glass of port wine after the big dinner and fall asleep immediately. Indeed the entire stock of Christmas booze consisted of a dozen Guinness, a half bottle of Jameson whiskey for visitors, a bottle of port wine and many bottles of raspberry and lemonade and a mineral with the strange name of Vimto, all stored under the stairs until the big day.

In their culture and time anybody who drank was suspect, to be pitied or condemned in direct proportion to amount consumed and behaviour resulting. Once a distant female cousin of Mr Toner landed a fiancé and brought him along to be introduced to the family. They bought in six Guinness in honour of the match. The children watched, astonished, as the fiancé finished all but one of the bottles. Mr Toner dutifully sipped the last one. When the happy couple left, their parents exchanged knowing glances: the marriage was clearly doomed.

Dinner was outstandingly good: no limit to the amount of raspberry lemonade you could drink and a paper cracker between every two people. Mr Toner was taking a photograph with a delayed action switch and they all screeched at him to hurry up or he wouldn't be in the photo. But he dashed back to the table in time. After dinner Mrs Toner had her glass of port wine and dozed off in the chair beside her mother and father. The older children did the washing up while the young ones listened to the orchestra of snores in the sittingroom and played with their toys.

The only blot on the day was when young Johnny took a shine to Dominic's train set and Dominic couldn't hit him because the adults were around, so he started crying in frustration. Granny Hope woke up and sorted out the row. Then she went back to snoring.

There was a lull then until teatime when they had turkey and ham sandwiches, more lemonade plus the Christmas cake with its almond icing. Then they all listened to the comedy show on the radio with Maureen Potter and Jimmy O'Dea.

Later they had a singsong round the piano until their grandparents were picked up by Mr Coyne to be brought home. Because of their early start that morning they were all exhausted and needed little pressure to go to bed, particularly as the following night which was St Stephen's night they knew they would be really late.

Every year Mr Toner bought eight tickets to the Queen's pantomime. Apart from maybe the rare musical film with Nelson Eddy and Jeanette McDonald – *Maytime*, which made them bawl, or *The Phantom of the Opera* which frightened them – this was the only time in the year he brought them all out. This wasn't surprising because each of the pantomime tickets cost two shillings and sixpence, which was a fortune.

It was an astonishing treat. The very act of getting the bus at Orwell bridge at seven o'clock in the evening when they should really be at home was exciting. There were girders narrowing the Orwell bridge which were called tank traps and which were barely wide enough to let the single-decker 47A bus pass through. The occasional daredevil driver would go through it at full speed. Surely in the dark some night the bus must crash into the girders? If it ever did, none of them was lucky enough to be on it at the time.

The pantomime was always hilarious apart from the stupid bits where they sang romantic songs. Mick Eustace was their hero. He only had to look imploringly upwards with his big white eyes and invoke his oul' fella with the mock prayer 'May the light of Heaven shine on him' and they were convulsed. Gloria Greene was the Principal Boy and had great legs, which occasioned constant winking and nudging when they were sure their parents' eyes were not on them.

The plush seats, the smoky atmosphere, the sweets passed from one end of the row to the other, the uninhibited roaring at Cecil Nash the villain, the rare glimpses of their own father grinning – this was life at its most perfect.

It didn't last, of course. Nothing did. They never forgave the Abbey Theatre for getting itself burned or the snobs that ran it for taking over the Queen's Theatre and depriving them of their annual treat.

– And all they put on there is smut by that renegade, O'Casey, said Mr Toner. Sure what would he know about the slums of Dublin!

Even the bus home had its excitement. They had landmarks to identify, particularly the brilliant Bovril sign changing colours up on the building at the corner of D'Olier Street and Westmoreland Street. Then there was that four-faced liar, the Rathmines town hall clock, which they could always confirm was lying by pestering their father for the correct time.

Walking in the rain down through a quiet Smokey Hollow was a pleasure. They could see the lights in all the windows except the poor Fennells, point out that nobody had a Christmas tree like theirs and smugly think of all their pals who hadn't been to the pantomime. And the fun was not over yet. They could look forward to a game of sevens and a singsong, with no pressure on anybody to go to bed.

But that Stephen's night was even more exciting. As they approached the Circle, they saw figures splashing through water. The Dodder had overflowed again! They ran. The water had come right up to their doorstep and entered the hall. Weren't they lucky not to be snobs with a carpet? Their linoleum floors could be easily cleaned. But what about the unfortunates down the road where the flood must surely have reached their mantelpieces? Good old Snotty Oliver's bulldozer – his model T Ford – would be ruined and it served the oul' crank right. Mr Toner filled a sack with clay and pressed it against the ventilation holes under the door step, although he admitted it was locking the stable door after the horse had bolted.

All the neighbours were out, rushing around like ants from under a disturbed stone, cursing the Corporation that had done nothing all these years to prevent such floods. Years later the Corporation would line the river banks with concrete walls in the hope of converting the torrent into a demure stream. It did no such thing.

Meanwhile the children joined in their parents' frantic mopping up with cloths and buckets and basins. Of course young Johnny was half dead with sleep and started whinging so Mrs Toner brought him up to Dineens' to spend the night. That made him worse. He whinged that his Mammy would be drowned and they had to bring him back.

They were lucky. The water hadn't done much damage although Mr Toner muttered ominously about the lake that must be under the floorboards. Nobody knew whether the river was still rising so they all stayed in the sittingroom until the early hours, and Mr Toner sang 'Old Man River'. They had a competition to think of all the songs they knew which were about rivers. They came up with 'The Volga Boat Song', 'Swanee River', 'Shenandoah' – pronounced Shannon Door, but it was still a river – 'Cruising Down the River on a Sunday

Afternoon', a Negro spiritual about crossing the Jordan. It was amazing how many they could think of. Mr Toner did his impersonation of Paul Robeson:

'You keep goin' your way,
I'll keep goin' my way,
River, stay way from my door.'

Mr Toner rounded it off by telling them a ghost story in which he was involved. It happened on a dark winter's night when he was walking home down the Green Lanes and a big black thing jumped over a hedge and chased him. They were transfixed with fear right to the end when the big black thing caught their father by the leg and started pulling it ...

– Just as I'm pulling yours, he ended.

As a matter of fact, they were all very relieved at the ending. Eventually the all-clear was sounded and they went to bed. It was a new world record for staying up late. Still, they rose early the following day to survey the river and the mess it had left. A coating of brown slimy mud covered the familiar garden and path. Secretly they wished that the rain would never stop so that they could have another night of excitement. Of course the rain stopped, but there were still some delights left. The bottom half of the Hollow was still flooded and the fire brigade came to pump the water from the street. They got a raft and paddled down to the end of the road with bread and milk for the people besieged in their upstairs rooms who lowered buckets and bags on ropes to receive the supplies.

On the way back Bern spotted something moving in the gutter and thought it was a rat until he saw a silvery flash. He reached over and scooped a fat trout onto the dryish part of the path. It was the first Dodder trout ever caught in a gutter and they had it for breakfast the following morning.

The river was still in spate and they could look from their bedroom window and see the trees and branches and dead dogs being rushed along on the brown flood. And of all things, they would remember the corpse of a big grey horse, its belly bloated, its brown teeth grinning, its eyes still staring as it was irresistibly jostled along in the rush to the sea.

– I don't see what it has to grin about, said Joe. But it was a great end to Christmas.

· THIRTEEN ·

WHEN MR TONER STARTED TO GO BLIND he was given sick leave from the brewery. He had already given up making barrels. 'It's a young man's job,' he said. He then spent a period as a smeller, that is, a man who went round sniffing at returned casks to make sure they were sweet enough to put fresh stout in. It was a very responsible job, he said, and required a nose like a bloodhound. You could ruin sixty gallons of porter at a go if you had a cold in the head. After that he was promoted to foreman and had to spend hours in the evening muttering over grubby cards. These were covered with his copperplate writing – lists of the names of men to whom he must allocate tasks the following day.

To the children, he seemed to have a poor opinion of his fellow workers because he spent the time crossing out and rewriting, using a rubber to wipe out names, saying 'Feck it, can't rely on him' and 'No, he's a malingerer' and 'Dammit, I can rely on nobody.' He was only a Number Three foreman, Mrs Toner explained to the children, because he spoke his mind too openly. He refused to softsoap anybody so he would never go any further in the job. The neutral way she said it made them unsure what should be their own attitude to this aspect of his personality. Was she making excuses for the lectures, the tongue-lashings he gave them? I have trodden on people's toes all my life, trying to shock them into awareness, their father would declaim. You needn't tell us, thought several of his children.

His crankiness was bad enough for short periods in the evening and at weekends. But the latest development – the sick leave – was disastrous for the children. Bad enough for him to be ordering them around when he came home from work, but to be there all the time! They wouldn't be able to get away with anything.

Mrs Toner was equally perturbed. 'How will I manage with him under my feet every day?'

The neighbouring wives shook their heads in sympathy. They knew what it was like when their husbands were stuck in the house in between jobs. A wife could let the house fall apart during the day as long as it was reasonably neat when the lord and master came home for his tea. One gigantic effort at about five o'clock usually sufficed.

But if he was there all day he would expect the same standard of order all the time and a woman couldn't possibly spend the day running after kids clearing up their mess.

For the Toner children, too, the personal tragedy came second to the social inconvenience. It would be very awkward, they decided, to have an oulfella going around with a white stick. They would have to spend day and night protecting him from other kids who would trip him up or call names after him. They knew this jungle better than their father. How could he know anything about the merciless predators round here when he always had his head stuck in a paintbox or a newspaper?

It was the survival of the fittest, nature red in tooth and claw: big fellows bullying little fellows, youngsters just out of nappies making cockshots out of mongrels, mangy dogs chasing cats, infants pulling their tails, the cats scratching infants, babies bawling, kids being blamed for it, mothers clattering kids, brothers pulling sisters' hair, sisters scratching them back and so forth. Mr Toner said that nature had a savage grandeur which could only be transformed and transcended by beauty and the eye of an artist, but his children lived in the real world. They weren't saints or artists. They simply wanted to survive without too many ridiculous rules and regulations.

His enforced holiday was bound to interfere greatly with their present, however circumscribed, freedom. He was already half-deaf and very cranky. What in God's name would he be like if he went blind!

There was a passing academic interest in whether it was worse to go blind or deaf.

– Sure he's half-deaf anyway.

– That doesn't stop him singing. Even if he was stone deaf he could still paint. That'd keep him happy.

– No it wouldn't. How would he listen to music?

They were silent. They knew in their hearts and souls that total deafness would be catastrophic for the man. He constantly quoted:

'Music, the greatest good that mortals know,

And all of Heaven we have below.'

What would he do if he was deprived of Galli Curci's 'Song of the Swallow' or Chaliapin's 'Song of the Flea' or the quartet from *Rigoletto* or the sextet from Lucia De Lammermoor or McCormack singing the 'Old House and the Fairy Tree' or the Immortal Trio from Faust or 'Some Soldiers Love the Leg of a Duck' from *Il Trovatore*? He had even started learning a new song he heard from Peter Dawson called, ominously, 'The Blind Ploughman':

'... God who took away my eyes,

That my soul might see.'

It would be better if he went blind, they decided. But how would he paint, then? How would he go off cycling down to Glendalough? At night, when they joined in the renewed and infinitely longer rosary they couldn't make up their minds whether to pray for his ears or his eyes.

He explained it to them when they asked.

– It's like a mist creeping in from the sea at the corner of this eye, moving across, over the bridge of my nose and starting on the other eye. Say this corner of my eye is Lambay Island. The mist comes in from Dublin Bay and covers it up, then it moves in over Howth Head and that's gone, vanished. Little by little it moves in until Dublin has disappeared and everything is black.

– But what started the mist?

– God only knows. A storm at sea, maybe. I just got a sudden pain. One day it was all clear. The next, there it was.

No connection was made with the fact that he and his wife

were cigarette smokers, a habit they continued. Sometimes he smoked the pipe too. They loved the smell of that and watched in fascination as he cut up the Yachtsman's plug and stuffed it in the bowl. It was a Petersen's pipe, of course!

– The thinking man smokes a Petersen pipe, he exhaled contentedly.

The smell of cigarette smoke was homely. The children loved it and were enthralled by the perfect smoke rings he could create. He could blow one ring and while that was expanding, blow another smaller one through it. Smoke was also used by Mrs Toner as a primitive air freshener. She always smoked in the lavatory which was known as the House of Parliament because they all had a seat in it. When there was a queue for the House and somebody was overlong in it they would be shouted at through the door: Hey, do you want a spanner to work it out? It was also a good place to have a sneaky drag of a cigarette.

Everybody smoked in those days. It was the initiation into manhood and that didn't stop little chisellers trying it out, even though they knew it would make them sick. Down at the end of the river path they congregated with butt ends salvaged from their parents.

– Give us a drag.

– Would you give me a chance. I only had one puff.

– Go on, you mean cunt, you have it half-smoked.

– It was only a tiny butt.

When it was so small as to be impossible to hold anymore without burning the fingers, a pin was produced, and the butt was impaled and sucked. As the nicotine was concentrated in the very end, this gave a lovely dizzy feeling. It also made them sicker. But nobody could admit that.

Kids who acquired a full cigarette and didn't share it were just lousers. One smart aleck, when he got a whole cigarette, always cut it up into three pieces and singed the ends. 'I've only a butt,' he would say apologetically as he placed the morsel between his lips. They became suspicious because he always had the same length of butt in his mouth. They could never prove anything but they nicknamed him Roy Rogers, i.e. quick on the draw. He knew very well what they were saying about him but he brazenly maintained the habit.

The way a person held a cigarette showed their personality as well as their status in life. If they held the glowing end inwards towards the palm it meant an adult had a menial job and was afraid of his boss catching him smoking. In a child it meant he was afraid of his parents spotting him. If the cigarette was constantly in your mouth it meant you were a fan of Humphrey Bogart. If you could smoke without coughing you were considered competent. If you could blow it through your nostrils like a bull you were really advanced. A girl who smoked was completely abandoned.

The smoking culture was the breeding ground for strokes and heart attacks but people hadn't yet been frightened into making the association. The blame was always laid on the Orwell Hill, 'the widowmaker', which everybody pedalled pantingly up if they were late for work or school. And deaths always came in threes, the women said. So everybody smoked on. 'It's a mug's game,' Mr Toner would say as he puffed away.

He spent hours checking the progress of the mist in his eyes, holding up a card in front of one eye and moving it slowly across. When it came to a stop he would grimace at his wife and put the card away.

Because he had little better to do he went to ten o'clock mass every morning with Mrs Toner.

– We're storming heaven again, she said.

Mr Ryder, his old singing friend, cycled over from Rialto with a present: a packet of cigarettes. But they weren't Players, Mr Toner's normal brand. They were a fancy cigarette, very expensive, called Passing Cloud. Mr Ryder didn't smoke at all which was why he could sing so well. Mr Toner was very touched by this gesture and the two friends' singing that evening had an extra bit of feeling. Mrs Toner brought in tea and marietta biscuits to them.

They all had to adjust to the new lifestyle. At least Mr Toner spent a lot of time in his shed in the garden. There he took to carving a barge out of three huge lumps of wood which he bolted together. It was a model of one of the Guinness boats. He got the measurements correct by cycling down to the docks and wheeling his bike up and down the dock beside the boat and then across its deck. He explained that he knew the circumference of the front wheel so all he had to do was mark the tyre with chalk and count the number of revolutions. They were extremely impressed by this practical application of arithmetic.

He spent months on it, creating the superstructure and funnels out of tin from cigarette boxes. He made the rigging perfect in every detail. He even put a little engine in it so that it actually chugged along when they tried it in the bath. It was so good that it won first prize in the annual arts and crafts show organised by the brewery. That was the year Bern entered a drawing and the Lord Mayor of Dublin, Mr McCann, was so impressed that he had him called over the loudspeakers and gave him a special prize of five shillings. It was also the year a real film star named Movita appeared at the sports with a boxer named Jack Doyle who beat her. Respectable people didn't stare at the couple but the kids couldn't take their eyes off her waxen face.

The prizewinning barge was brought home in triumph but instead of handing the model over to the children to be played with and probably broken – isn't that what toys are for? – Mr Toner hung it up on the wall to be admired.

His constant presence round the household made them tread warily. It cut down on the number of audible squabbles in the house. But it only shifted the battlefield outside. Dominic once had to organise an ambush down at the river with Paddy Murtagh because he couldn't scream and kick at Joe who was making his life unbearable. Joe wasn't doing anything out of the ordinary, just being older and overbearing. Paddy and Dominic waited for a long time by the bank, armed with the stalks of umbrella plants, but Joe never came.

It was an unnatural state of affairs. These things would normally be worked out in five minutes at home and then forgotten. Mr Toner's presence meant an unhealthy suspension of hostilities.

That was until the episode of the reflector. Joe bought a new reflector for the back mudguard of his bike. He was very proud of his bike, which was a sports model and which he kept immaculately clean and shiny. It was the envy of everyone. The reflector was to be the finishing touch. Joe made two mistakes. One, he told nobody about the purchase, wanting to have it fitted before he displayed it to the world; second, he left it lying on the bench in the shed on the very day Mr Toner was doing something else.

It so happened that Bern dropped into the shed shortly afterwards and spotted the new reflector. It was just lying there. It must be one his father had discarded because he wasn't cycling anymore. It was exactly what Bern needed for his wreck of a bike. He hesitated. It looked a bit new for his father to discard. In fact he knew that Mr Toner found it impossible to discard anything, old or new. Mrs Toner said he was a magpie. Mr Toner said: Waste not, want not.

Suppose it was somebody else's? Well whoever it was must be very careless just to leave it lying around. Anyway, there was one important rule of the jungle that everybody knew: finders keepers, losers weepers.

He hesitated no more, took the reflector and fitted it to his own mudguard. He surveyed it: a perfect fit. There was the little problem that it looked a little too new for his bike. He rubbed dust over it. Better. But it still looked out of place. Sure, who'd notice?

At teatime all hell broke loose. Joe burst in.

– You stole my reflector.

– What reflector?

– What reflector! Don't act innocent. The new one I bought this morning from Jimmy Lee, the one you put on your bike.

– What are you talking about? I've had that reflector months.

– You're a dirty liar.

Mr Toner dropped his newspaper. Ominously.

– What are you two on about?

– He stole my new reflector. He's a dirty thief.

– That's a serious accusation. Bern, did you take something from him?

Bern was outwardly calm. Normally the accused could brazen his way out of these things, deny everything for a while, have a slagging match, maybe a bit of a scuffle and then return the property or not, depending on how persistent the accuser was. The ultimate decision of the accused would also have to be measured against what had been lifted from him previously by the present plaintiff. A kind of violent barter system operated in which some kind of crude justice emerged.

This was different. How could Mr Toner in his righteousness know the inbuilt balances and tensions that kept the system going? Bern was worried. Last time Joe had stolen a penny from their mother Mr Toner had exploded, pulled all the money from his pocket and flung it in the air, bellowing: 'This stuff is not important. Honesty is.' After a terrible silence that situation was defused by young Johnny saying, tentatively, 'Da, if you don't want it can I have it?' Then they all collapsed in laughter. But there mightn't be such a safety valve now. Mr Toner was bound to introduce another abstract concept like Justice in capital letters and turn this private thing between Joe and himself into a battle between the forces of good and evil. He would never let nature take its course.

Bern had no alternative.

– I don't know what he's talking about.

Joe was so livid that he overlooked the fact that this wasn't a normal squabble. The Supreme Court was listening to every word they said.

– You fecking liar. You know exactly what I'm talking about. You stole it and put it on your own bike and rubbed dirt on it to make it look old.

Bern was still calm.

– Would you listen to him. You're raving mad.

Mr Toner crushed his paper. That was a bad sign. The others went quiet.

– That's enough of that. Come out the two of you. I'll settle this.

They trooped out to the shed. Joe rubbed his finger against the reflector, held it up to show the dirt.

– That doesn't prove anything, said Mr Toner. It's just your word against his. Now if somebody's stolen something they better own up this instant or there'll be murder.

He turned his glare on Bern who adopted a wide-eyed innocent look and sank deeper in the quagmire.

– I never touched his reflector. If you don't believe me, look at the initials.

They bent down and inspected Bern's initials which were indeed cut into the rubber surround of the reflector. Even Joe was taken aback.

– That seems to be the end of that argument, said Mr Toner, glowering at both of them. It better be, he added.

They went back into the house to finish their tea. Joe softly whispered at Bern:

– I'll get you, you bollix, I swear.

– That'll be enough of that, said Mr Toner and straightened out his paper noisily.

Joe confined his attack to dark looks at Bern, who assumed a nonchalance he did not feel.

Later that evening Joe came into the diningroom where everybody was sitting peaceably around.

– Are you still saying that's your reflector?

Bern looked up from his homework.

– Are you still on about that?

Mr Toner looked warningly over the top of his newspaper. Joe was now the cool one.

– How do you explain this?

Joe carefully unwrapped a piece of paper and displayed the contents. Mingling with the dust were a few tiny, newly cut slivers of rubber, the same kind of rubber as on the reflector.

Bern said nothing. Mr Toner asked:

– Where did you get those?

Joe never took his eyes off Bern. He spat the words out.

– I've been down on my hands and knees for the past hour, collecting them from the floor of the shed.

Mr Toner took the piece of paper, screwed up his good eye

to scrutinise the contents. He handed it back to Joe and looked at Bern.

– Go upstairs you.

He may have been half-deaf and going blind. Perhaps it was frustration at his growing infirmities. There is no doubt that Bern, the eldest, always got the worst of things. The eldest is always the one the parents practise their mistakes on. But the thrashing he gave to Bern that night was felt by all. Even Joe looked a bit sick at the sounds coming from upstairs.

And then Mr Toner stopped going blind.

Mrs Toner said it was prayer. Mr Toner jokingly said it was the Passing Cloud cigarettes that Mr Ryder gave him. He had gone for his weekly check-up to the Guinness dispensary, the terrible place where their mother brought them all to have teeth pulled by a savage in a white coat. The smell of hops from the surrounding brewery and the wet cobblestones between the high buildings were always associated with toothache.

The doctor shone a light into Mr Toner's eyes and frowned.

– I would have thought it was irreversible, he said.

The general consensus was, as always, that the weekly novena had saved him. The children had one concern.

– Will you be going back to work, Daddy?

– You can't wait to get rid of me, isn't that right?

They shuffled.

– No, that's not what we mean.

– Well all I can say it'll be a blessing to get back to the peace of the brewery.

Life resumed its normal course.

· FOURTEEN ·

'THE MAN WHO SITS ON A REDHOT POKER
IS SURE OF AN EARLY SPRING...'

Mr Toner would sing as he prepared lazy beds for potatoes in the small back garden on St Patrick's Day. Not that this interested Dominic, who hated spuds.

He couldn't stand the little black bits, the discoloured areas that persisted even when they were peeled and cooked. Worse, Mrs Toner refused to cook them soft saying all the good would go up in steam so they had to eat them hard. The same applied to potato skins in which most of the nutrition was supposed to be located – a theory which always emerged when Mrs Toner got fed up peeling enough spuds for eight mouths. Lumpy, discoloured spuds so dismayed Dominic that he often feigned sickness so he would not have to eat them. If there was no escape he would crush them into the edge of the plate, camouflaged, as was the custom, with knife and fork.

His father said it was a throwback to the Famine when the potato let the Irish people down and he said Dominic was a perfect example of the folk memory. This explanation was a great temporary relief to Dominic but it didn't work when he used it in his father's absence, and his mother clipped his ears and told him not to be cheeky, she'd give him folk memory.

Yellow was for Easter which was on its way. Buttercups shared the same intense colour. They used to hold them under each other's chins to see if they liked butter. The statues were all covered in purple velvet in Holy Week when they went to do the seven churches. This was another certain way of getting indulgences, a kind of spiritual credit stored up to be set against future sins. But you needn't cod yourself that they would save you from hell. Indulgences were useless there. With a bit of luck like a deathbed confession you might avoid hell, but once you went there, you were a complete goner. Indulgences were useful only for shortening your time in Purgatory, which was just as hot but you knew it wasn't a life sentence. The greater the number of indulgences, the shorter your stay in Purgatory.

So they didn't mind doing the seven churches for these and other reasons ... mainly other reasons. There was no other pretext on which Hollow parents would allow a gang of their offspring to rampage unsupervised through the city, getting up to all kinds of divilment. For instance, would the Hollow kids ever have had the chance to see a real live corpse, as they put it, if their parents were in tow? No fear.

It happened in the Hospice for the Dying in Harold's Cross. They had said their six Our Fathers, six Hail Marys and six Glory Be's in Rathgar, Rathmines, the Perpetual Adoration place in Fitzwilliam Street, Clarendon Street, Whitefriar Street and had only two more to do so they were on the final straight towards Mount Argus and Terenure. As they passed the Green-mount Oil Company at Harold's Cross bridge, Slag Kelly stopped the gang with his hand in the air like an Indian scout.

– Hey. What about the Hospice? he said.

– That's not a church.

– Of course it's a bleedin' church. Don't they have to say mass there for the dead people!

The others were doubtful.

– Would it count?

– Well, it's going to count for me. We do this, then Mount Argus and we can skip Terenure. I'm fed up walking anyway.

They agreed with this. They'd had their fun, going along the Rathmines Road and knocking on five consecutive doors and seeing the owners popping their heads out one by one like a series of cuckoo clocks while the kids ran like hell towards the copper dome of Rathmines Church. They had called on the Toners' mad Aunt Maggie, Granda Toner's sister with the motheaten fox fur on her shoulders and the hairnet over her red-grey curls. The Toners were a bit smug about this because nobody else had a mad aunt and she would only let her relations in to the flat. But they didn't stay long. Her biscuits were always mouldy.

Bern, Joe, Ginty and The Slag had successfully scutted on the platform of a tram in Rathmines, watched admiringly by the girls and the smaller kids. They had lit a candle without paying for it in Whitefriar Street which was a sin but it would use up only a tiny bit of the day's indulgences and they were feeling expansive. They'd had a brief but bloody shooting war with Bang-Bang who ambushed them from the platform of the 16A. They had exchanged insults with Maggoty Mary, the old woman who always stood cursing outside Rathgar church, hoping she would coin some new obscenity to be stored up for future use.

In fact, they'd really done everything that was appropriate to the day that was in it. The suggestion of shortening the pilgrimage was welcome.

Trying to look respectable they streeled after The Slag into the grounds of the Hospice. He swaggered ahead up the driveway and ducked to the right, through the trees until he led them to a solitary round building. The door was open and they wandered in to a cool, dim place where there were beds arranged in a circle. They looked around for the altar but there was none. When their eyes got used to the subdued light they saw the beds were made of marble and there were monks asleep on them. At least they looked like monks. They had brown habits on them and big rosary beads entwined in their white fingers.

– Jasus, they're dead, whispered Slag Kelly.

The girls and the younger kids started backing out but stopped when they saw that Bern was actually approaching one of the beds. He touched a pillow tentatively, then looked back at them wide-eyed.

– It's made of marble, he whispered.

Their expressions encouraged him to further daring. His finger approached the cheek of the corpse. He touched the yellow stretched skin and said, 'Whew'. It seemed safe for the others to subdue their nervousness and approach the corpse nearest them but always keeping a safe distance. Eventually they were all drifting between the slabs, calling each other: 'Hey, look at this one, it's a woman' or 'Gawd, you'd think they were only asleep' and even making jokes. In the middle of this scene they heard a rustle and the door opened. They jumped as a nun swooshed in and started screaming at them.

– How dare you! What business have you in here! Have you no respect for the dead? Get out of here.

They were already on their way, running, as she screamed inconsistently after them:

– Come back here this minute. I want your names. I'll find out what school you're in. Never you fear. You'll be taught respect. What kind of parents have you ...

They ran, half-carrying, half-dragging the younger ones who were in a state of terror.

– Wouldn't you imagine they'd give the poor divils a real pillow on their deathbeds, said Bern when the company had recovered its composure halfway up the Rathgar Avenue.

– Them nuns are mean rips, said Slag Kelly. He looked around to make sure the girls weren't listening and said: They wouldn't give you the steam off their piss.

– I nearly got frostbite touching the face of that corpse, said Bern.

– Go on. You didn't touch it.

– I did so.

– I was watching and you didn't, said The Slag, who felt he'd been upstaged.

– Well, if you don't believe me ... said Bern loftily.

– Okay. Okay. Have it your own way. You touched it. But I bet he died of a contagious disease, said The Slag cleverly. That shut Bern up.

There didn't seem to be any point in doing the last two churches so they went straight home and told their mothers they'd done all seven churches. Not a single mother believed them.

Good Friday was a terrible day. They had to go to the church again and file up to the altar to kiss the crucifix laid on the sanctuary steps. The radio was silent, the piano was locked and it was the most boring day in the year. But come twelve noon on Saturday they could all relax and look forward to Easter eggs and the sun dancing on Easter morning. It was nearly worth the awfulness of Holy Week.

Birdnesting was the main excitement in spring. They knew that if you took all the eggs at one go the bird would abandon the nest because she would smell their hands. To take one egg was all right. But then if everybody took one egg there'd be none left and the bird would leave anyway, so what was the point in being abstemious? Better to have two or three in case one got broken on the way home or during the delicate operation of blowing them: a pinprick in each end, then a gentle puff and the liquid would flow gently out unless they had been picked too late and there were youngsters inside. That happened often.

Nevertheless Bern accumulated a fine collection of eggs. The golden crested wren's was the prize, the smallest bird and the smallest egg in Europe, he said. It was acquired from a perfect nest in one of the pine trees in the field across the Dodder and it took him hours of meticulous care to blow it safely. When one of his brothers smashed the collection in a rage, that was the only one he mourned.

The Healions, the fatherless family down in the cul-de-sac, were known to be great egg collectors too, preferring the blue speckled eggs of the blackbird because, it was rumoured, they used them for omelettes. They were too poor to buy real eggs. There was also a song about one of the daughters of the house:

'Minnie Healion sells fish,
Three halfpence a dish,
Cut their heads off, cut their tails off,
Minnie Healion sells fish.'

They were so poor that Mrs Healion was reputed to use cocoa on her legs to simulate the latest rage: liquid nylon stockings. They waited in vain for her to come home in the rain so that they could witness disaster. Others hinted darkly that she should have no difficulty getting real nylons from visiting sailors because she wore Clery's knickers which had the slogan

'One yank and they're down' printed on them. This was a crude adaptation of the well-known litany of a Clery's sale: 'Ladies panties down; Big things in men's trousers ...'

Spring was also the time for 'docking' or 'foxing' dogs. Granda Hope said that if you didn't dock a dog when he was a pup all the strength would go into the tail and the dog would grow up a weakling. He advised going to Mr Visser, a well-known fisherman who was also gatekeeper of one of the big houses on the Orwell Road. He would be better than a vet because all vets were robbers. Visser wouldn't charge a penny because he was a friend of Granda's.

They brought the latest pup – there was a regular turnover of dogs in the household – up to the gate lodge, curious to see what was involved. Some of the kids said Oul' Visser simply bit the tail off; others that he tied a piece of string tightly round it and left it there until the piece rotted and dropped off. But apparently he had different techniques for different breeds because he did neither of these things.

He instructed them to hold the animal firmly on his workbench. To their dismay he took out a hammer and chisel, placed the latter on the dog's tail and took a swipe at it. The howls of the pup seared their minds. Mr Visser shouted at them to hold still, placed the chisel once again on the bloody mess and this time severed it completely. He bound the red stump with a cloth and they carried the whimpering animal home, all of them feeling sick. The dog survived. The effect on the dog was easier to assess than the damage to their own sensibilities

The dog's name was, of course, Scamp. All successive dogs in the Toner household were called Scamp. Once a policeman demanded the current dog's license from Dominic who told his father who called to the police station and reassured them that this dog, like the others, was a stray and really didn't belong to them.

For Dominic, the relief at not being thrown into prison was tempered by regret that he couldn't ever say 'It's my dog' again. But Mr Toner said that nobody could own an animal or a human being. You could only look after them temporarily.

Everything belonged to God. There was no arguing with that. Only Bern had the temerity to suggest their father had told a fib to the police. Mr Toner suppressed his natural impulse to lash out and explained that it depends on how you put something. For instance, De Valera, 'the greatest parliamentarian in Western Europe', was seen smoking on a retreat, a religious weekend. A pal of Dev's said he himself had been refused permission to smoke during meditation. Dev said that he had asked the wrong question. He should have asked was it possible to meditate while smoking. They were all impressed by that and learned the basic principle of situation ethics.

One of these transient dogs taught Dominic a lesson. He brought it up to Pogue's Valley to act as Lassie in a re-enactment of the famous film. The game went well at first with all the kids calling out 'Lassie come home' and whoever the dog approached was the winner. But then somebody got bored because there was no shooting and said he was going to be Johnny Mack Brown.

So absorbed were the children in arguing that Johnny Mack Brown was a cowboy and had no business in a Lassie film that they didn't notice the pup wandering away. Dominic forgot about it and came home. Months later he was thrilled to see the pup, now grown into a dog, on the banks of the Dodder. He rushed joyfully up, calling out 'Scamp, Scamp'. But after a polite acknowledgment the dog ignored him. Dominic, rebuffed and shocked at the animal's short memory, swore that his next pet would be an elephant.

The lengthening evenings enabled them to come out to play after tea. Because it was still chilly the best games were physical, like skipping. Two would swing the rope. The rest would queue up to take their turn. Whoever tripped was out. The last survivor had to keep skipping as the rope was turned faster and faster: 'Salt, mustard, vinegar, pepper, fresh garden tea' or 'Chase, chase, chase the hairy elephant' until the last child could keep it up no longer.

The more leisurely games were accompanied by street songs.

'Somebody under the bed, whoever can it be?
I'm feeling very nervous and call for Maura Lee.
Maura lights the candle, nobody there
Hee-hi-diddley-eye and out goes she'.

A great one for the more romantically inclined was when
one girl stayed in the middle and the others joined her for one
skip before exiting:

'There stands a lady on a mountain.
Who she is I do not know.
All she wants is gold and silver
And a nice young man to know.
Who's your lover, who's your lover,
Who's your lover, fair maid.'

Whichever boy happened to be caught on the last line had
to go with her behind a hedge to do what he or she could with
a barrage of jeers following them. The best Dominic ever got
from this was Breda Lynch who allowed him a few puffs of her
asthma cigarettes which tasted horrible. He preferred the
brown paper fags he and his brothers smoked on Saturday
mornings when their mother was at the shops.

The children took over the Hollow street on these elastic
evenings, prattling, gathering, dispersing like the sparrows on
the wires, crowding together like notes from their music books.

Games contributed to their literacy. They would try to memorise as many film titles as they could from the newspapers.
Then they would take turns to write the initials in chalk on the
pavement. Whoever guessed the title was 'on' next. Young
Johnny nearly got lynched one evening for writing T.F.O.T.O.
and causing them to waste the short twilight trying to decipher
The Phantom of the Opera.

Only the boys could play the tyre-rolling game because if
the girls curled up inside it and allowed themselves to be rolled
along like a hoop, people would see if they had dirty knickers.
But they could all play parachutes with their fathers' stolen
handkerchiefs. You tied a string to each corner, joined the
strings to a stone, folded the whole thing neatly and flung it as
high as you could. The hankie would open and float gracefully

down unless it was trapped in the overhead wires. In the parachute season you could see fathers standing at their gates, fuming up at the wires and trying to identify their snotrags.

Spring was also frustrating. Although there was brilliant sunshine it was still too cold to swim. Their Granda still called out 'Damn the weather' and the milkman still wore a glove on the hand in which he carried the churn. This contained horse-piss according to those who were not his customers but it seemed mostly all right to Mrs Toner who always insisted on a 'tilly' or an extra splash when he had filled the pint container. She said it was the only way she could get value because the blackguard definitely watered the milk.

Mr Leary, the man with the Corporation dustcart, never discarded his thick muffler whatever the season because they said he had throat cancer which looked very ugly. He wore fingerless gloves as he scooped up the horse droppings. He was a very ill-looking man. Mrs Toner always stopped to have a word with him, because her husband lusted after the dung for his garden. Mr Leary regularly wheeled his odoriferous load into the back garden and tipped it over. She was instructed to give him a shilling for a pint as a reward but he didn't drink so they often wondered why he was so obliging to her. It must have been that they found enjoyment in discussing each other's ailments so pleasurably.

Spring was also a pain because after the Easter holidays there was the endless period in school before summer. June was a nightmare, watching small white clouds in blue skies through the high windows of the national school. The sadists who built these schools made the windows too high for child-ren to see anything that might distract them from study. If the planners had thought of small white clouds there would have been no windows at all.

Summer was there when the stepping stones on the river were completely uncovered, when the tar on the roads became soft and you could extract a piece and roll it into a perfect ball to be kept in your pocket for future reference or until your mother came screeching in, holding up your ruined shirt and demanding: What kind of a careless brat were you, how was she supposed to wash melted tar out, did you think clothes grew on trees, was she made of money, was that the thanks she got for slaving day and night, wait till she told your father ...

But summer was perfect. They could escape from the house and its chores and spend all day swimming in the brown water of the Dodder. At least the boys could. No girls were allowed to swim there. It wouldn't be ladylike to undress among those crude young fellows. It would be like a girl whistling or smoking, things that Our Lady never did.

So the boys had perfect freedom. Even when it rained it didn't matter. You could put your clothes under a bush, dive into the spattered river and debate whether it was wetter in or out. On really hot days they could stay in their togs from morning to night. They even wore them home for their meals and escaped immediately afterwards in case their mother remembered things they had to do.

The river afforded three grades of places to swim. For beginners there was Alcock's Hole, a shallow pool just behind the Toners' back garden wall. It had overhanging branches which allowed pygmy Tarzans to practise. Mr Toner taught most of the kids to swim there, having rehearsed their strokes on the kitchen chair or in the bath where he encouraged them to hold their breath for as long as possible. That was the secret of swimming, he said, which was why the Toner kids spent a lot of time swimming underwater before they realised all they had to do was stick their heads above the water and they'd be swimming properly. He forgot to tell them that.

Next was the stretch directly above the waterfall for slightly older children. This was also good for sunbathing because you could walk across the waterfall and sunbathe on the ledge of the old mill house and sing:

'There was a man named Michael Finnegan
He grew whiskers on his chinagain
He shaved them off but they grew on again
Poor Old Michael Finnegan.'

This was intended to enrage a little girl named Finnegan

who lived just across from the waterfall and couldn't get at them because her mother wouldn't let her near that dirty river. The girl was unpopular – her nickname was Fungus Face – but her back garden had the best pear tree for miles around and one or two of the boys overlooked her plainness to benefit from its munificence. Others disdained such deceit and simply stole from it. The latter had a double sense of glee when they were invited into the garden to play legally. Harriet sensed she was being used. Hence her fury at the song.

A hundred yards upriver was The Bridge, the senior section. Here the accomplished swimmers and divers spent the day showing off their prowess. They graduated from wild leaps to bellyfloppers to smooth jack-knives off the crooked tree on the right bank, then the high wall on the left bank. The penultimate step was to dive off the ledge on the bridge itself.

Only men would take the ultimate step and dive like the Toners' English cousin from the parapet itself. The best diver ever was a man named Craddock who used do jack-knives and somersaults from the bridge until one day he came up with his head embedded in a watchman's brazier and they nicknamed him 'The Man in the Iron Mask.'

The children from the Hollow made sure to be there first thing in the morning, before the crowds came. At this time the water was crystal clear, the sun was at the perfect angle and they could dive for the tin cans that became Long John Silver's doubloons. Eels only came out at night so they had nothing to worry about. The first to dive in would surface and yell, 'It's like soup', and the others would follow quickly, to emerge cursing him, saying that it would in fact freeze the balls off a brass monkey.

The day progressed gloriously towards the heat of the afternoon when they stretched out on the footpaths of the houses fronting the river. There they competed for the best tan. Dominic and Joe took the sun so well that they were often asked were they Indians or had they a touch of the tar in them. Bern suffered a bit from sunburn which meant he spent most of the time dashing across the road to plunge in and cool off.

They lazily studied the movements of the odd small cloud which always seemed to head for the sun. They would forecast the dimming and then shout, 'Come out McCormack'. Why 'McCormack', nobody knew except that was the name of a famous singer who was a star and therefore in the firmament. It seemed a feeble explanation, but who cared in the mind-damping heat.

The houses whose footpaths they cluttered with their bodies and shabby towels were the better-class facade of the Hollow. In summer the ghetto spilled over and the planners' deceit was exposed; no discreet suburb this, but a teeming hive of wiry bodies. Most of the residents endured the invasion with bad grace. Those who objected strenuously were treated to a clear footpath. But on both sides they had to run a gauntlet of little boys holding their noses and going 'phew' when the house-holders passed in or out.

On these days the children pitied people who had to stay in their clothes: unfortunate parents, sisters and very small kids. The occasional priest, nun or Christian brother who passed by in their suffocating black clothes confirmed the impression that religion was a mug's game, only for cold winter days. Many a potential religious vocation was successfully resisted on these grounds, lost in the summer haze.

Adults were rare in this group. All fathers had jobs and mothers stayed at home. They were keenly aware of the occasional stranger who might stop at the bridge to lean over and study the brown bodies. If he was respectably dressed he was automatically regarded as a potential dirty old man, a nancy-boy, and treated with circumspection. Jokes about homosexuals were many and harsh. Innocence was scorned. Children repeated references whose meaning they could not possibly understand. They learned prejudice like the ten-times tables, by rote. It was assumed that only people with fancy accents, who 'talked proper' engaged in this disgusting, if mysterious, activity. In this respect, at least, they preserved a certain innocence.

Oddly, they tolerated one young man who never swam,

always strolled by fully dressed and wore a cravat, not a tie. His nose was always stuck in a book. He was tolerated because he said he was a poet. Poets were sissies all right, but they weren't nancy-boys, so he was accepted without jeers. Even when he put on his snooty, highfalutin' accent they didn't mind; poets had to be a bit crazy. When Bern asked him what book he was reading, he replied that the word wasn't 'buke', it was 'buk'. It wasn't even a 'buk'; it was a novel. That put Bern and the rest of them in their place. They challenged him once to recite a 'pome' and he quoted something he said was his own, about the enviable daring of the wind that could press itself against a girl's thighs and get away with it without rebuke. They thought that wasn't bad. It proved not only that he was what he said he was but that he wasn't what at first they suspected him to be.

On the rare days when the sun did not shine there was fishing, a twenty-four hour occupation because of the night lines. Joe was the expert and regularly came home with a big slimy eel draped over his shoulder, the fish dangling lifelessly because he would have beaten its head against the wall. But chisellers didn't know that so he had great fun chasing them, waggling the eel and frightening the life out of them.

Joe always skinned the eels and Mr Toner used the skins as bandages for sprains. He would wet the skin and as it dried on the wrist or ankle it would squeeze tighter, effecting a speedy cure.

Parents had mixed feelings about the river. It was undoubtedly a marvellous amenity. It kept the children out of the way and nobody ever drowned in it. The worst that ever happened was somebody falling in, or more likely being pushed, fully clothed. That happened regularly. So parents ignored the occasional dead dog that floated down. There was plenty of water to dissipate any potential disease.

Still, Mrs Toner tried to bring them as often as possible to the health-giving sea. She thought it would counter the potential maladies from the river. Polio was common at the time, as was tuberculosis, scarlet fever, asthma, rheumatic fever and the rest. It must have worked, because the Toner kids never contracted anything fatal even though they sunbathed with the rest on the Fever House, an odd concrete structure reputed to be the point where the Corporation sewage pipes intersected. Sandymount Strand was the nearest strand but it was not handy as they had to get a tram and a bus and still walk miles. Even then they usually had to walk a long way out to get enough water to cover their ankles. The tide was always out on Sandymount Strand.

You could never get a decent dive there and as that was the principal purpose of swimming the strand was a dead loss. Finally, unknownst to Mrs Toner, it defeated her purpose entirely because much of the sewage from the city found its way there.

The true seaside was Bray. You had to go there by train.

· FIFTEEN ·

BRAY WAS TO THEM WHAT THEIR FATHER was always singing about: Nirvana. For one thing it was miles away from the Hollow, an exotic place that even had a speed limit to make the English visitors feel at home. It tried to be as much like Blackpool as possible and had dodgems, lights on the mile-long promenade, candyfloss, chips, clock golf, boats for hire – too expensive for them – vulgar postcards and decent waves.

Getting there was nearly as good as being there. They had to get a train from Milltown. It meant crossing the stepping stones just over the back wall, running through the field with the avenue of pines, coming out at the Dartry dye works whose clock told them whether they were early or late for the train. Halfway down the long hill they passed the other waterfall, more a weir, which their father had painted. They argued with each other about whether the cows in the picture had moved.

– Don't be stupid, said Bern, how could they be the same cows. He painted it last summer.

But in high summer it looked unchanged. It certainly felt the same: motionless green scum above the weir, a little dribble leaking over, the trees as leafy as the picture itself.

At the Dropping Well pub the seven arches of the high viaduct came into view and the older ones began inching ahead, to be called back by Mrs Toner. She seemed to spend the entire day counting them, telling them to tie their laces, mind them sandwiches, hold the milk upright or it will curdle, come in off the road, don't walk in the gutter, stop teasing, hold the younger one's hand, if you don't come back this instant we're going home, and not another word out of you.

Milltown station had roses that didn't look as if kids were

let near them. You had to cross over a high metal bridge which was great for spitting down from onto the tracks. Stop that filthy habit, their mother would say. She really had eyes in the back of her head. Would anyone have the nerve to stand on that bridge and spit on a train as it passed underneath? You'd have to time it perfectly. Otherwise you'd be suffocated by the smoke.

It was impossible to relax – I'm warning you, stay away from the edge of that platform, a man was killed here once – until they were on board and the door of the carriage was safely shut.

– I'll break your neck if you touch that handle again, she said.

The children settled down to look for familiar landmarks.

The first was their uncle's grave in Dundrum cemetery. They could easily spot the glass cover of the tiny statue of the Blessed Virgin and get their mother to recount once again, in detail, the manner of his death at the hands of a football. The fragility of people was brought home. It still fascinated Dominic although he knew he would have his nightmare again. He was almost getting used to it. As he grew up he would look forward to it almost as much as the one where he was flying.

They were silent as they watched the world moving at an incredible speed outside. The silence was broken by Bern.

– Heynimanoosh, he muttered.

They pricked up their ears.

– What?

– Heynimanoosh, he repeated.

– What's that mean?

So he told them about a film he had seen in the Classic where a man on a train said 'Heynimanoosh, heynimanoosh' and it sounded like the wheels of the train. People around him picked it up until the whole train was going along whispering 'heynimanoosh'.

They tried it out and it was true. Of course they couldn't keep it down to a whisper and eventually they were screeching out 'HEYNIMANOOSH' until Mrs Toner said stop it or we're getting off the train at Shankill. So they shut up for a while.

Outside the tunnel in Dalkey the train stopped to let another train pass on the single line. The silence before the other train swooshed by was enormous. Then Joe noticed the blackberries, enormous juicy ones leaning towards the carriage window, unpicked because of their inaccessibility. They looked in utter frustration at them until the train jerked and moved off again.

Because trips to Bray were expensive they were infrequent and so never lost their novelty. The narrow Albert Walk between the station and the promenade was like Aladdin's cave. Buckets, spades, funny hats, slot machines – catch-pennies, their mother said – were all beyond their slender allowance of a penny each for the day but they could enjoy the sheer pleasure of the unattainable. A fool and his money is soon parted, she said.

Some of the delights were free. They could linger behind and covertly study the racks of postcards with fat women and skinny little husbands. Their mother pretended not to notice them smirking at all the little willies, the slipping bikini tops, the huge bottoms and purple noses, all the colourful innuendos about drunkards and peeing and kissing and other great gas from a different world.

Bray trained them for life. The waves were smashing but the pebbles hurt their feet. The one ice-cream their mother bought them was delicious but melted too soon. The salad sandwiches and hardboiled eggs always, no matter how careful they were, became nests of sandy grit. The tea on the grassy prom was perfect, but Mrs Toner never stopped complaining about the robbers in the houses fronting the promenade who charged a shilling for a kettle of boiling water.

– I mean, look at the Corporation workers who ask me for boiling water outside my door. Do I charge them? I know what they'd say if I did. The world is full of thieves.

The bandstand had a fenced enclosure where women in flowery dresses and men in straw hats sat just like in the postcards and listened to jokes from bright young repertory actors which sounded like the postcards, too. The children could never understand why people paid perfectly good money to get into this enclosure to hear the bands or see the actors when you could see and hear them perfectly well from outside the fence. But as there must be some advantage they did their level best to sneak past the man with the leather bag at the gate. He easily repulsed them. They decided the people inside were just snobs and left it at that.

Mr Toner missed a lot of fun in Bray. He was always working. They would have loved to have him there. Mothers were great fun at making the picnic but it would have been great to have the oulfella there too, not as a father, mind, but just as a male adult vaguely on their side. He might even cough up the odd few pence for an extra ice-cream.

On one occasion the four eldest climbed Bray Head on their own and sat at the top looking down at the pygmies on the promenade. It was a still day and they could hear the music from the prom drifting faintly across the water. It was Bing Crosby's latest:

'Mersey Dotes and Dozy Dotes
And liddel lamsey divey,
A kiddley divey too,
Wooden you,'

which, because they were well up on these things, easily translated as 'Mares eat oats and Does eat oats and little lambs eat ivy; a kid'll eat ivy too, wouldn't you?' They hummed along quietly ...

As far as they could remember he accompanied them once only but it wasn't much use because he disappeared up the Bray Head to spend the day painting. Oulfellas were difficult to fathom, especially oulfellas like their oulfella. He was good at things like dribbling a ball or doing press ups and he knew all about swimming and things, but he seemed to lose interest very fast. Maybe they bored him. Oh well, shag him, Bern said and invented all kinds of games which he was best at, of course, but still they were games.

The one time Mr Toner joined them in Bray – it had to be a Sunday – he treated them to tea and chips in the Edenmore

Hotel. It cost one and threepence each – minimum charge, no reduction for children – and was the first time they had ever eaten out.

– Now listen, said Mr Toner. We're not tinkers. Any shenanigans and we leave.

They were nervous at being in a hotel. The woman with the red hair who greeted them loudly made them cringe and realise they had a terrible cheek being there. This was for other people. Their father cleared his throat and gave the order for tea and chips. The woman asked in a loud voice: 'Will that be all?' and they felt embarrassed when he said 'yes'.

Jesus God, why weren't they rich enough to buy the oul' bitch out like they did in the comics? They would all come in from the limousine with the uniformed chauffeur, with pound notes bursting out of their pockets and cigars bristling from all their mouths, even the baby's, their mother in a fur coat, their father wearing a silk top hat and penguin suit, calling out: 'Give us double portions of everything and a barrel of lemonade.'

Mr Toner frowned at their muttering. They lowered their eyes. Mrs Toner kept the baby quiet. Warfare over whose napkin, knives and forks; chairs too near each other round the small table, elbows in the way, imagined faces being made – all was conducted in total silence.

– I could eat a horse, Mr Toner said heartily.

– Did you smell her breath? whispered Mrs Toner

– There's nothing like the fresh air to give you an appetite, he said, giving her a frown.

– There's a stain on the tablecloth, she said.

The corner of his mouth said:

– Would you give your arse a chance.

Someone, probably Bern, giggled. She destroyed him with a look.

The people on the other side of the small room were not loaded with togs and towels and cups and the detritus of a picnic. The two men wore white shirts and pants with the crease in them; the women had new-looking flowery dresses.

They were red-faced and spoke quietly in funny accents like their English cousins.

The chips were soggy and Mrs Toner made gestures of derision but her husband gave her a warning frown. This was a Hotel, after all. The children's hunger made them not notice. They ate a little more carefully and much more silently than they would at home. But they still cleared the plates.

– Luvly kids, one of the red-faced men smiled across the room.

Mr Toner swallowed his last chip hastily and put on his affable look which was a half-hearted grin.

– You don't know the half of it, he said.

– Enjoy them when they're young, said the man. Ours are too big to come on holidays with us. Luvly they are, kids.

– Ah sure, said Mr Toner. They're grand when they're asleep. Come on the whole shooting gallery of you. Gather your paraphernalia.

He paid the bill carefully, Mrs Toner having vetted it to make sure they were not overcharged.

– God bless now, said the people at the table.

– Enjoy your holiday, said Mr Toner.

The children trooped out, exchanging opinions.

– Nice people, said Mrs Toner.

– Never trust an Englishman's smile, said Mr Toner.

What chance had they got, indeed.

The worst thing about Bray was having to leave it while the sun was still high in the sky over the Sugarloaf mountain.

Ah c'mon, just one more dip, they would plead. I won't tell you again, Mrs Toner would say. Normally she would have to tell them over and over. But with Mr Toner there was no malingering. Slowly they set off for Albert Walk. It was awful having to leave this paradise to rich people from England who could afford to stay in hotels and guesthouses. They decided that the kids who actually lived here must die young, of delight.

Still, there was always the train home. The older ones stuck their heads out the window to see Bray Head receding, the sunlight running away over the sea towards Wales – you can see it on a fine day, said Mr Toner. The lone figures on Killiney Beach: who were they? Remote, like people in films, no kids, just dogs.

– See Naples and die, see Killiney and Bray, said Mr Toner.

– Hee-haw, hee-haw, they chorused dutifully. It was one of his few jokes.

They always tried to stay at the window until the last moment before the Dalkey tunnel engulfed them with a roar, risking the smuts from the engine getting in their eyes. One was always too late.

– Oh, me eye!

– I warned you. What did I tell you? Will you never learn?

– It's paining the life out of me.

– What do you expect? Here, show me.

– I'm gone blind.

– Would you hush. It's only the tunnel.

The grit was carefully removed with the corner of a hanky.

– Now, do as I say and close that window.

They subsided, watching the telegraph poles whipping past, Bern trying to estimate the speed of the train by working out the distance between the poles and counting them as they passed. He worked out a hundred miles an hour which impressed them very much. Their father was humming:

'When the golden sun sinks in the west,
 And the toil of the long day is o'er.
 Mm mm mm mm mm mm.'

They noticed the effect of the setting sun on each other's faces.

– Hey, you've got yella janders.

– Shurrup.

– I'm only telling you.

– Mammy, tell him to stop.

– I'm warning you ... is that the thanks we get for bringing you out? Squabble squabble squabble.

– He started it.

– I'm warning you. Dry up.

They would then subside into a chorus of 'Heynimanoosh,

heynimanoosh, heynimanoosh,' quietly so they wouldn't give her another headache. What did she think on these trips? Did she have reference points beyond the duties of child-rearing? Yes: God and his Blessed Mother kept her going except for the occasional lapse when she found herself pregnant again when, as she admitted much later in confidence, she had walked to Rialto Bridge with the intention of throwing herself in.

– Heynimanoosh ...

– Never take threats like that seriously, dismissed Mr Toner. Women are always complaining.

Nothing like that disturbed the sheer pleasure of the train. The children were full of history, bragging about the number of dips they had had, what they had seen that the others hadn't, whether the dog that ate the discarded sandy sandwich was brown or grey, to whom did it belong – the man with the walking stick or the owner of the ice-cream kiosk? Did the pebbles reach beyond the waterline? Precisely how high were the waves? Who was in first? Who was out last? Had the others seen the man who swam miles out and just treaded water for hours until they thought he couldn't make it back? Who (whispered) had seen the woman when her towel slipped and her bum was exposed? I did. You did not. I did so. You did not, you liar. I did so. Okay, what colour was it? The towel was red. Smart aleck.

– What are you two arguing about?

– Nothing.

– Well stop it, my head is splitting.

They made passionate vows about what they would do on the next visit. There was no disagreement here. Indeed, they incited each other to greater flights of fancy.

Then a last quiet chorus of 'Heynimanoosh'.

The walk from the station in Milltown back to the Hollow was the worst part. The heat of the day made the evenings comparatively chilly. Mrs Toner and the girls pushed the go-kart in front and the boys trailed behind, quiet, nursing their thoughts. Mr Toner took up the rear like a sheepdog, humming all the while.

If only they could have a real holiday where you didn't have to go home in the evening. The Murtaghs went to Bournemouth every year; but they only had two kids. The Dixons had relatives in County Kildare whom they could visit. The Toner kids had no relatives in the country even though their Granny was born in Drogheda and Granda Hope came from Tibradden in the Dublin mountains. But they were so old they had no relatives living. Even if they had, who'd take on six kids? It was hopeless. Still, Bray made up for a lot.

· SIXTEEN ·

MR TONER ON HOLIDAY MEANT THEY HAD LESS FREEDOM than usual. He spent some days working in the garden and it took great dexterity for the children to slip out unbeknownst to him. If he spotted them, weeding was their fate. Other days he would set off early on his bike, paintbox strapped to the crossbar, raincape folded over the handlebars, not to return until evening. He would spend the rest of the evening humming in the sittingroom, rendering the sketches of the day into watercolours of mountains and lakes and scenery. If they chanced to enter he would launch into a lecture on the beauty of God's nature and ould guff like that, so they gave him a clear berth.

Sometimes they went for bicycle trips. Once he brought them to the source of the Dodder. It was an unimpressive dribble.

On Sundays they all went up to Kilmashogue, the mountain at Tibradden behind Rathfarnham where Granda Hope came from. But even their mother didn't know where his house was. The younger ones were carried on the crossbar and carrier of their parents' bikes. There was a lot of walking on the way there because it was mainly uphill. There was nearly as much coming home because Mr Toner didn't trust the brakes on the bikes. He was an awful worrier.

It didn't deter Joe and Bern who would swoop on ahead, heads bent low over handlebars, pretending they were speedway riders. They'd catch up on girl cyclists wearing slacks and yell 'Emptyfork' and the girls would screech back 'Take more than youse to fill it.'

The picnics on the hill were great. The smell of bracken fires lingered forever and they could have wars with goat shit, the tiny hard balls which they pretended were shotgun pellets. Some were fresh and soft, however, so the girls hated playing. One time they caught a baby rabbit and brought it home. Mr Toner built a temporary hutch of wood and garden wire but the rabbit was gone in the morning. There were dark hints about rats and otters and foxes which made the youngest cry.

The worst was when he took them to the National Gallery on a Sunday.

– Would you for God's sake try and keep up. I can't be waiting all day for you. Are any of you listening at all?

The children threw last, lingering glances at the marble statue of naked lovers which dominated the first room of the gallery.

Reluctantly they streeled after Mr Toner. The statue was a great opportunity to study anatomy but he seemed to sense it. Ever since the Sunday he caught Joe fiddling with the man's mickey, saying he was a williechecker, Mr Toner hurried them past. The kids giggled but he wasn't amused.

– You'll have us all put out of the gallery. Come on. And pay attention. You might learn something.

His peremptory whispers dragged them away, to continue the aimless traipsing through big, echoing rooms, he waxing eloquent about art and something called chiaroscuro. He showed them every picture of the crucifixion and triumphantly said they were all painted wrong: the nails should be through Christ's wrists, not his palms.

– Would you look at that? Look at the hands. Now look at your own. If a nail went through there it couldn't support the weight of your body. It has to be through the wrists. So-called artists. They know nothing about anatomy. Now Da Vinci, he's a different kettle of fish. He knew his stuff.

It didn't make much difference to them; the pictures were all boring. But there was an echo in all the big rooms that wasn't bad. You could hear whispers and footsteps of people who weren't there at all.

Anyway how could he be right and all the pictures wrong?

163

Every time they saw a picture of Jesus he had blood on his palms. Even the one in their Granny's where he was fully dressed and carried a lantern knocking on doors to call some unfortunate to heaven. And what about Theresa Neuman that he was always talking about in Germany or somewhere? Didn't her hands pour blood every Easter! Didn't he say she was a saint in her own lifetime! He couldn't have it both ways.

It was more interesting what he said about Jesus's loincloth.

– Idiotic! It should be tied round the cross too. It wasn't put on for modesty. They didn't bother about things like that in those days. Weren't they all Roman pagans? The loincloth was to hold him tight to the cross.

Try as they might they couldn't imagine their Blessed Saviour up there without even a shirt to cover his mickey. It was funny thinking of him having one at all. Did his mother always have to be telling him to stop playing with himself?

There were piles of things in the gallery, most of them a terrible pain. All right, there was the huge picture which must have taken years to paint which showed Cromwell's soldiers killing women and children in Drogheda. That wasn't bad, a bit like a film in the Classic, huge and plenty of blood but all the tits and things covered up with bits of clothes. You could imagine them, last thing before they died, men, women and children, dragging their clothes across to hide their yokibusses. Still, weren't they always told that modesty was the greatest virtue. It went back a long way.

They paused over a piece of ivory which Mr Toner said a Chinaman had carved thousands of years ago. It was like a latticework sphere and through the holes you could see a little ball inside, made of the same colour ivory. How did the ball get in there?

– He cut holes in the ivory first and then, through the holes, he carved the ball.

They looked in wonder.

– Can you imagine the patience. It took him years. He had to cut away with a little sharp knife everything inside except that ball. Study it. That's art. No good for anything. But wonderful. Nobody knows who he was. Just a little Chinaman, working away, minding his own business. His missus must have thought he was mad. Sure maybe he was, too.

He gave his wispy grin and marched on.

Out in the bright afternoon sunshine of Merrion Square they blinked and wished the Dodder wasn't prohibited on Sundays. Remember that thou keep sweaty the Sabbath day. Even if they could have a run around the park in the square itself. But Mr Toner said it was locked because it belonged to the Archbishop of Dublin. Renegade Catholics and begrudgers said the Archbishop kept it because it was valuable, but the Archbishop was a man who always did good by stealth and he was going to build a Catholic cathedral there because the Protestants had stolen all ours and all we had was an imitation one – the procathedral. They half-listened. Who cares on a sunny day?

Finally their prayers for a real holiday were answered. One of the visitors to the house, a friend of their father's, was the gardener of a big house in Churchtown. They were all allowed to call him Pat so they never learned his second name. He wore a cap and had a protruding jaw which made him look like a chimpanzee when he laughed. No matter what anybody said he would reply, 'Thass right', so Thassright became his nickname. His bicycle was the tallest they had seen, what they called an upstairs model, a big black-framed machine which he pushed with one hand. When he rode straight-backed and tall like a ship in sail the kids shouted: 'Get down and milk it' or 'Is it cold up there?' Thassright always smiled back.

His employer was Mr Lambton and he called to the house a couple of times. They were enormously impressed because he had a motor car and Mr Toner said he was a decent man for a Protestant. Mr Lambton took an interest in their father's painting and said he envied him his gift. Then he asked Mr Toner to paint a picture of his big house. It must have been the only professional commission Mr Toner ever got.

Their mother told the girls that Mr Lambton had been a suitor of hers before she was married. They weren't sure what were the implications of that and didn't waste much time thinking about it either. Lambton was a Protestant, wasn't he? Nothing could have come of it.

The fee for the their father's first commission was astronomical: the use of Mr Lambton's holiday bungalow at the seaside for as long as they liked. It was unbelievable. The bungalow was forty miles away in Brittas Bay at a place called Ballymoyle, County Wicklow.

The three youngest travelled with their mother on the train from Milltown. The others left early and cycled all the way with their father, rucksacks on their backs and necessary supplies tied everywhere. There were good reasons for this: it would toughen them up, they would see a bit of Ireland and finally, they would appreciate the bikes when they got there. The nearest shop was three miles away from the bungalow.

They were waiting at Arklow station when the train travellers arrived.

This was posh. An ass and cart and its owner had been hired to carry the luggage. The ass was reluctant to move with the weight of people and luggage and its owner was at a loss until Joe copied Granda Hope and yelled at the ass, 'Hup ya bitch', and kicked it. Mr Toner pretended not to notice. But the ass did. It moved.

It was the last leg of an amazing journey, the furthest anybody had ever been from home – barring their parents' honeymoon, but that didn't count. They had never seen culchies in their native habitat before.

– Look at them gawking, said Bern.

Every window and door had somebody staring at them.

– Sshh, said Mrs Toner.

– Gawk Street, said Bern, and they all laughed. They were on their holidays.

Ballymoyle was twice as good as they imagined and would be ten times more wonderful when they remembered it. All they had to do in the morning was jump out of bed, don their togs and roll over and over down the sand to the magnificent blue sea. The wooden house – it had a wooden verandah too – was perched on top of a sandy cliff which would years later be so eroded that the structure tumbled into the sea. Even at that stage it looked perilous and they accepted their parents' exhortations to go easy when they chased each other round and round the house.

They spent all day, every day on the strand which stretched as far as the eye could see. They couldn't remember a boring day in the two glorious weeks. Even the terrible thunderstorm, when they huddled safely under the covers and occasionally peeped out to see the lightning over the sea, was exhilarating. When their father could be enticed away from his sketchbook and easel he swam with them and they found his white body, as usual, incongruous. But he gave lessons to those who couldn't yet swim, mainly, he said, because there was a dangerous current here and they'd better be able to look out for themselves.

Dominic would never forget the feeling when he realised he was staying on top of the water. It was much better than when he had to hold his breath, crawling along like a submarine listening to the great suck and swish of the pebbles. Not that he hadn't always enjoyed that too, the feeling of being absolutely alone in a strange world, a change from the noisy company of his siblings. Mind you, it was reassuring to see the odd arm or leg nearby and know their splashing would frighten away the conger eels. But this levitation was certainly better. He dreamed of flying that night.

Mrs Toner never swam. She sat in a chair on top of the dunes, knitting. Somebody had to mind the baby, she said, and do the cooking and cleaning, too. But she only complained once.

– I might as well be at home, for all the holiday I'm getting. At the end of the day I'm still worn out.

Mr Toner tightened his face and said nothing. Not wanting to cast too much of a damper, she shrugged.

– Still, a change is as good as a rest, I suppose, and the air will do us all good.

They relaxed a bit then and continued foraging for the wild strawberries among the dunes.

One day the inflated football bladder which they had

brought as a beachball was caught by an offshore breeze and moved relentlessly out to sea. Bern, being the best swimmer, decided to pursue it.

He didn't realise the tide was also receding and he moved very fast away from shore. They shouted to him to be careful but the noise of the surf carried their voices away. They shouted until their father came running, paintbrush still in his hands, and let out such a roar that it would crack glasses like that singer did in the film. They must have heard it in Arklow town. The children had never seen such an expression on his face as he dashed into the sea. It wasn't his ferocious face. They had never seen this face before. Not on him, anyway. Fathers are not supposed to look frightened.

Bern turned. He must have heard the shout. He saw them waving and realised the distance he had come. He started to head towards them. Their mother heard the roar too and stood up, hand to her mouth.

It took Bern a long time to make progress and he had slowed even further when their father reached him and had to push him the last few yards. They both stood up in the shallows and Mr Toner manhandled the boy up the beach. The rest looked forlornly out at the ball bobbing its way towards Wales.

– That was an idiotic thing to do, said their father gruffly to Bern. He always said 'idiot', never 'eejit' like everyone else.

Bern began to explain in great detail, as was his wont, but Mr Toner just ignored him and marched off down the beach towards his easel.

The only visitor they had was Thassright. He came on his bike, still wearing the big black coat while they were in their togs. He and Mr Toner set off one afternoon on their bikes into Arklow and didn't come back for hours. When they finally arrived they pretended to be drunk and staggered up the path, their bikes weaving in front of them. The kids roared laughing and even their mother hid a grin.

– Would you have a bit of sense, the pair of you, she said.

They instantly sobered up, whether they were drunk or not. In the evenings they had one last walk on the beach before bedtime. Mr Toner led the way, declaiming the beauties of God's creation and quoting lines of flowery poetry while they straggled behind or rushed ahead – but not too far because when the sun went down the sea and the caves looked not quite as harmless. He showed them how anemones squirted and pointed to the parasitical hermit crabs. The sandflies rose like locusts as they approached and settled again immediately they passed. They saw a bat one evening and covered their throats because they had seen a Dracula film and knew what bats did for food. They mastered the art of skimming flat stones on the water and he told them a scientist had used that technique to drop bombs on a Nazi dam. That's right, they'd forgotten there was a war on.

He showed them how to make a spark in the dusk by striking two stones together.

– Are these the right stones?

– There's only one way to find out.

– Ah, I can't do it.

– Here, you're not holding them right. You have to hit them hard. And mind your fingers. There. That's the way the cavemen invented fire.

– Had they no matches?

– Don't be idiotic.

There was no electricity in the bungalow so those who could read did so by candlelight or torch. Bern and Dominic were the bookworms. At home they often ignored their father's warning about going blind and read under the covers with the aid of a bicycle lamp. They found *The Last of the Mohicans* by James Fenimore Cooper in the house and began to read it simultaneously. It was all right during the day when one could pick up while the other was busy elsewhere. But at night in bed was awkward because Bern was far advanced in reading ability. They hit on the solution of lying on their stomachs, with the book in between, each holding the page they were at. Time ran out for Dominic. The holiday was over before he could finish the story.

They nearly missed the train from Arklow because the ass

and cart was late and still moved in slow motion. Finally Joe took over, shouted his magic formula and whipped the animal to get there on time. Because they were leaving the area – possibly forever – they made faces back at the curious faces on Gawk Street.

When they got home the first thing to do was dash out on the street and brag. Dominic met Paddy Murtagh who had again been in Bournemouth. They matched experiences like card players, but Dominic had the trump card: he could now swim on his own. Paddy couldn't top that so he changed the subject.

– Did you see the plane?
– Which one?
– A big bomber.
– Course I seen a bomber.
– Not this one you didn't. It wasn't near Arklow.
– How do you know?
– I know.
– What about it anyway?
– There's a big bomber just dropped the biggest bomb in the world.
– Where is it?
– I don't know. But they're going to drop another.

Curious, the two small boys scanned the calm, blue evening sky and saw nothing except the highflying swallows which meant that summer was going to continue forever.

Other Books from The O'Brien Press

LAND OF MY CRADLE DAYS
Recollections from a Country Childhood
Martin Morrissey

A touching and informative evocation of growing up in County Clare during the war years, superbly written.
A book of pure entertainment that is also a rich and valuable social record.
Through the eyes – and ears – of a growing child this book brings us to the heart of life in rural Ireland as it was lived before modernisation. *(Paperback)*

'Enchanting stuff - the outpouring
of a true storyteller'
THE CORK EXAMINER

REVOLUTIONARY WOMAN
Kathleen Clarke 1878 – 1972
AN AUTOBIOGRAPHY

Sensational first-hand history
written by an activist.

Kathleen Daly Clarke lived through and was part of the revolution that transformed Ireland from a British colony to a modern state. She was an activist and an early champion of women's rights.

In her own words she tells about the 1916 Rising and the executions which followed, including those of her husband (Tom Clarke, President of the emerging Irish Republic) and her brother (Ned Daly); she gives an account of prison life with Countess Markievicz; of the Civil War and first Irish Parliament and the politics of the Irish Free State. (*Hardback*)

'Richly satisfying' THE IRISH TIMES

GREAT IRISH WRITING
The Best from The Bell
Ed. Sean McMahon

The Bell was a famous literary journal, edited by Sean O Faolain and Peadar O'Donnell, wherein one found all the major names of contemporary Irish writing. Sean McMahon has selected the best articles from those journals and put them together in book form. *(Paperback)*

'As nearly perfect a balance between the contrasting talents and the various forms of writing as one could imagine'.
THE IRISH TIMES